"I'm on the right track now, I think."

Clary went on to explain. "I'm really beginning to know what life is all about."

"Which is?"

"To be true to oneself . . . sounds easy enough but isn't."

Alistair received that in silence. Clary wondered what he was thinking. She said, "What is your guiding principle?"

"Not dissimilar to yours. To define what one wants and go for it."

It sounded quite different from her philosophy. "Go for it" had an aggressive, acquisitive ring.

Anne Weale and her husband live in a Spanish villa high above the Mediterranean. An active woman, Anne enjoys swimming, interior decorating and antique hunting. But most of all she loves traveling. Researching new romantic backgrounds, she has explored New England, Florida, Canada, Australia, Italy, the Caribbean and the Pacific.

Books by Anne Weale

ANTIGUA KISS
FLORA
SUMMER'S AWAKENING

HARLEQUIN ROMANCE

1512—THAT MAN SIMON
1629—A TREASURE FOR LIFE
1747—THE FIELDS OF HEAVEN
1848—LORD OF THE SIERRAS
2411—THE LAST NIGHT AT PARADISE
2436—RAIN OF DIAMONDS
2484—BED OF ROSES
2940—NEPTUNE'S DAUGHTER

HARLEQUIN PRESENTS

565—WEDDING OF THE YEAR
613—ALL THAT HEAVEN ALLOWS
622—YESTERDAY'S ISLAND
670—ECSTASY
846—FRANGIPANI
1013—GIRL IN A GOLDEN BED
1061—NIGHT TRAIN
1085—LOST LAGOON
1133—CATALAN CHRISTMAS
1270—DO YOU REMEMBER BABYLON?

Don't miss any of our special offers. Write to us at the following address for information on our newest releases.

Harlequin Reader Service
P.O. Box 1397, Buffalo, NY 14240
Canadian address: P.O. Box 603,
Fort Erie, Ont. L2A 5X3

THAI
SILK

Anne Weale

Harlequin Books

TORONTO • NEW YORK • LONDON
AMSTERDAM • PARIS • SYDNEY • HAMBURG
STOCKHOLM • ATHENS • TOKYO • MILAN

Original hardcover edition published in 1990
by Mills & Boon Limited

ISBN 0-373-03108-4

Harlequin Romance first edition February 1991

THAI SILK

Printed in U.S.A.

CHAPTER ONE

CLARY had lunch at Daret's, a popular eating place close to the Tha Phae Gate of the ancient city of Chiang Mai in northern Thailand.

There were tables inside, but most of the café's patrons—ninety per cent of them young foreign backpackers—preferred to eat out of doors, at the tables under the trees.

Two of the trees had handwritten notices nailed to them. One read 'No drugs here, please' and the other 'Attention! Don't purchase illegal drugs or other people may inform the police and end your vacation'.

Clary's lunch was a tropical fruit salad and a beer mug of *lassi*, a whipped blend of banana and yogurt. Afterwards she walked along the shady side of Tha Phae Road heading east, a tall, sun-tanned, capable-looking girl in shorts and a clean T-shirt, her hair tied back at her nape for maximum coolness in the broiling heat of early afternoon.

It was two o'clock when she reached her destination, the post office. In London it would be seven o'clock in the morning, a good time, she hoped, to appeal for help from an early-rising man she had never met.

A man who, from the little she knew about him, didn't sound a soft touch for anyone, least of all a girl whose troubles were largely of her own making.

The international telephone call office was off to the right of the counters selling postage stamps. The

cement floor and iron grilles across the windows were
an unpleasant reminder of the building inside the old
city where she had been that morning.

For a moment, in spite of the heat, she felt cold
with horror at the thought of being locked in there
for an indefinite period.

Several people were already waiting on the bench
opposite the counter. Clary gave the necessary details
to the clerk and sat down, wondering how long it
would be before it was her turn to enter the glass kiosk.

Already she had overspent her daily budget. The
long-distance call to London would probably use up
her allowance for the rest of the week, maybe next
week's as well.

But who else was there to turn to except this man
Alistair Lincoln? She hoped he had got out of bed
on the right side this morning.

Although she had rehearsed what to say, when the
moment came to speak to him she found her normal
self-possession had suddenly deserted her.

Her mouth dry with nervousness, she said, 'My
name is Clarissa Hatfield. Can you hear me all right,
Mr Lincoln?'

'I can hear you perfectly. But I don't remember
meeting you, Miss Hatfield,' was the crisp reply.

He had an attractive voice, but his tone held a defi-
nite note of impatience; as if, when the telephone rang,
he had been about to sit down to breakfast or had
even been on the point of leaving for work.

She said, 'You haven't. I'm calling on behalf of
Nina Lincoln.'

'She asked you to call me?' He sounded surprised.

'Well, no . . . not exactly.' Nina had given her his
number but said she would be wasting her time. 'But

someone has to help her and you seem to be the only person who can. She's lost touch with her mother and has no other close relations.'

'Nina is not my responsibility. Whatever problems she has, she'll have to sort them out by herself. She's a big girl now.'

'Nineteen isn't very old when you're in the kind of mess Nina's in, Mr Lincoln. She's in Chiang Mai prison... has been there for three weeks already.'

The man at the other end of the line wasn't easily disconcerted. There was no amazed silence, no startled exclamation. Without a pause, he said calmly, 'On what charge?'

'Buying pot from a *tuk-tuk* driver—but in fact it was someone else who bought it and planted it on her.'

'How do you know that?'

'Because she's told me the whole story.'

'Nina isn't renowned for her truthfulness.' Now his tone was sardonic.

'Mr Lincoln, this conversation is costing me at least two pounds a minute. I can't afford to discuss the situation in detail. I'm not even a friend of Nina's... but I can't see a girl of her age stuck in jail in a foreign country without doing something to help.'

'Give me your number and I'll call you back,' he said briskly.

'I don't have a number. I'm a backpacker staying at a guesthouse which doesn't have a pay phone. It's where Nina was staying before she was put in prison. I'm speaking from a public callbox.'

'What's the name of the guesthouse?'

'The Old Teak House, but——'

'I'll be there some time tomorrow. Thank you for calling, Miss Hatfield. Goodbye.'

He rang off, leaving her stunned by the speed of his decision to come to the rescue in person. Perhaps he was a kinder, nicer man than Nina made out or he had sounded at first.

After she had paid for the call, Clary left the building and walked slowly back the way she had come.

Visiting hours at Chiang Mai's gaol were from eleven to noon and from one to two o'clock on Tuesdays and Fridays. She had already spent an hour with Nina this morning and wouldn't be able to visit her again until Friday. But perhaps the prison authorities would allow her to send in a note telling the younger girl that Alistair Lincoln was on his way.

Clary was inclined to doubt his assertion that he would arrive tomorrow. February was a high season month in Thailand. Not only because it was the time of year when Europeans and North Americans wanted to escape from the cold at home. But also because December to February were the coolest and driest months in this part of Asia.

Foreigners—*farangs*, as the Thais called them—fell into three main categories: businessmen, package tourists and young people seeing the world on a shoestring.

Clary was in the last group, although at twenty-seven she was older than many of the backpackers.

High season meant that flights from Europe to Thailand and from Bangkok, the capital, to Chiang Mai in the north of the country were heavily booked. Even if he travelled first class—and according to Nina he was so rich that paying her fifty-thousand *baht* fine, about twelve hundred pounds, would mean nothing to him—it might not be possible for him to get on a flight immediately.

The old part of the city was a square surrounded by a wide moat which nowadays had well-kept banks planted with flowering trees. Within the moat there had once been a high brick wall of which only the corners remained, with some recent reconstruction of how it must have looked long ago when Chiang Mai, meaning New City, had been built in the thirteenth century, later to become the centre of the kingdom of Lan Na Thai, meaning 'million Thai rice fields.'

After crossing the east side of the moat, Clary stopped at a café where she ordered a glass of fresh orange juice and took out the spiral-bound notebook she always carried in her shoulder bag.

> Dear Nina, she wrote
>
> I have explained the situation to your step-brother. He is coming to Chiang Mai as soon as possible. If he's not here by Friday, and I shouldn't count on it because I hear that flights are heavily booked, I'll come and see you again. Meanwhile keep your chin up. I'm sure things are a lot more hopeful now that Alistair has agreed to help. As far as one can judge by a voice, he sounds very much the Action This Day type and the best possible person to tackle the situation. See you on Friday. Clary.

The note signed, she sat sipping the chilled juice and wondering how a man still only in his middle thirties—although at first Nina had spoken as if he were much older—had contrived to make so much money that a flight halfway round the world meant no more to him, financially, than a ride on a London bus to one of his employees.

Perhaps understandably, as it had been five years since she had last seen him, Nina had been vague about how her stepbrother had amassed his fortune.

Her mother, now in America, Nina wasn't sure where, had married her second husband, Geoffrey Lincoln, when Nina was a baby and Alistair was in his mid-teens. According to Nina he had always been jealous of them and gone out of his way to be unpleasant, especially after his father's death.

To Clary it seemed fairly natural that a teenage boy who had loved and lost his mother should, at first, view with disfavour his father's new wife and her baby girl. Adolescence was a difficult period at the best of times, and doubly so when loss and grief were added to the usual insecurities of that age.

She remembered her own difficult transition from childhood to womanhood. She could smile about it now, but had wept many secret tears and suffered many pangs at the time. It hadn't been easy being the only child of a man who would have preferred a son and a woman who had wanted a daughter as petite and pretty as herself.

Mrs Hatfield, now in her fifties, was still a pretty woman whose friends admired her dress sense and her flawless grooming. But she had never understood that the kind of clothes which suited her were not right for her lanky daughter and that the most skilful make-up would never make Clary pretty. She wasn't so plain that men ignored her. But her fine clear skin was her only pretension to beauty, and Bette Hatfield had wanted a blue-eyed blonde who would borrow her high-heeled shoes—she never had fewer than thirty pairs in her wardrobe—and numerous bottles of nail polish. Instead of which she got a gangling giraffe with mousy hair and eyes of the most ordinary grey, Clary thought with a rueful smile at the memory of Bette Hatfield's efforts to transform her.

A few days ago she had sent her mother a present: a dress length of lustrous silvery-blue Thai silk with a crocodile watch strap for her father tucked between the folds. Clary was fond of her parents, even though they had never given her the warm, unconditional love she had longed for.

At one time she had resented that, but her travels in the East had taught her that, compared with many children in Asia, she had had a privileged childhood. Even Nina, who had lost her freedom and complained that the prison food was uneatable and she was dying of boredom, was not as badly off as she thought. There were worse fates than being betrayed by one's boyfriend, thought Clary, who had a pretty good idea how Nina had felt when she had been left in the lurch. Something not quite as bad, but almost, had happened to Clary two years ago. She was over it now, had put it firmly behind her as a bad experience better forgotten. At least it had made her wiser about men and more understanding when Nina had told her about Sean, the man who had played such a rotten trick on her.

The prison on Ratwithi Road had high white walls with a guard keeping watch from a look-out tower at each corner. There were said to be four young *farangs* imprisoned at present, all of them charged with the same offence and all unable to pay the heavy fines which would secure their release. It was rumoured they could be kept inside for as long as ten years if they had no parents or other relations to come to their rescue.

A long time ago, in the company of trustworthy friends, Clary had smoked an experimental joint, had found it a non-event and never tried another. Her view of the drugs scene was that anyone dealing in hard drugs deserved to be shut away forever. As for marijuana, used moderately, she thought it less damaging than nicotine and no more harmful than alcohol. But she couldn't sympathise with people who carried it or bought it in a country like Thailand where the punishments for possessing it were known to be severe.

On her way to the prison she had the luck to see a smartly uniformed member of the Tourist Police, all of whom spoke some English and whose function was to help tourists in difficulties. He was on a motorbike. When she signalled to him, giving a respectful *wai* as his motorbike drew alongside, the polite gesture of putting her palms together and inclining her head made his face break into the ready smile of all the Thais she had encountered. She explained her errand and he agreed to come with her and interpret her request to the guards at the prison gate.

Afterwards she walked back to the Old Teak House, wishing it had a swimming pool in which to cool off. But only the big hotels catering to affluent tourists had pools.

She wondered where Alistair Lincoln would stay. The city had several expensive international-standard hotels, but on what it cost to spend one night in airconditioned luxury Clary could live for as long as a week. However, although her lodgings were not always comfortable and occasionally a bit squalid, in one way she was better off than the tourists in the ritzy hotels. She had plenty of time.

Most of the affluent visitors had only two or three weeks here, not nearly long enough to see all there was to be seen or to get away from the well-beaten tourist tracks. She had already spent nearly a year travelling in Indonesia and Malaysia and when she had had her fill of Thailand she was going to India to spend another twelve months exploring that great continent.

After that? She didn't know. The only certainty was that eventually she would run out of money and have to stop travelling and start earning her living again. But when and where that would happen, and what she would do when it did, she didn't want to think about now. For the time being she was free; free from the nine-to-five grind, free of all domestic chores except washing and ironing her few clothes, free of all emotional ties.

And in view of the outcome of her one and only love affair, Clary was determined never to repeat the experience, never to lose her heart again. If she married, it would be for companionship and children. Definitely not for love. She felt the same way about love as she did about malaria. She didn't want to catch it. To avoid the latter she swallowed two Paludrine tablets every morning with her tea, and a Maloprim pill once a week.

To avoid losing her heart again she was friendly only to men who didn't attract her. To those who did she gave a polite brush-off if they tried to chat her up. But when there were younger, shorter, curvier girls about, often they didn't notice her.

*   *   *

Twenty-four hours later she returned to her lodgings to find a message awaiting her.

She guessed who it must be from as soon as she saw the fuchsia-coloured Thai Airways logo on the envelope. Inside was a sheet of airline writing paper decorated with a blue and gold design taken from the wall of a temple.

On it was written 'I am staying at the Mae Ping Hotel. Shall expect you for dinner at 7 p.m. when we can discuss the situation in detail. Alistair Lincoln.'

'Did you see who brought this note, Suthipong?' Clary asked the daughter of the owner of the guest-house. She was a pretty and intelligent girl of fifteen, eager to improve her English which already she spoke well.

'It was brought by one of the porters at the Mae Ping Hotel. He told me it was from a very important and very rich man from your country who arrived today,' said the Thai girl. 'He must want to see you very much, this man, because he had already written the letter to you and the first thing he did when a limousine brought him from the airport was to order the message to be brought here immediately. Who is he, Clary? Is he in love with you? What does the letter say?'

The questions made Clary grin. Enquiries about age, income and other personal matters were not considered impolite in Thailand, and soap operas were as popular here as they were in the West. So it wasn't surprising that Suthipong, scenting a drama of some kind, preferably romantic, shouldn't hesitate to express her curiosity.

'No, I've never met him,' she answered. 'We've only spoken on the telephone. I shall meet him this evening. He's invited me to dinner.'

Suthipong looked concerned. 'But what will you wear? You have no nice dresses. The trousers you wear at night are not suitable for the Mae Ping. The ladies there will all be wearing silk dresses and jewels.'

'I have a skirt in my pack which will do,' Clary said. 'What made the porter think this man was rich and important? Did he give him a big tip?'

'He didn't tell me that, but he said the Englishman had reserved a suite in the Executive Club, which is at the top of the hotel with the best views. It costs thousands of *baht* to spend one night in those suites...more than most people earn for many weeks' hard work,' said Suthipong.

It was she who had told Clary about Nina's imprisonment and Sean's desertion of her. He had come to the guesthouse first. The next day she had arrived. A few days later they had gone hill-trekking together, leaving some of their gear behind in the care of Suthipong's mother. When they returned they had asked for a double room which they had occupied for a week, seeming very much in love, very happy. Then one day Sean had come back and said he was leaving because Nina had done something stupid and was in trouble with the police and he didn't want to be involved.

Suthipong's mother had believed him. She already disapproved of Nina for letting him sleep with her. Men were men and took what they could get, but good girls held out for marriage.

Suthipong was a good girl who intended to save herself for her future husband and looked down on

the girls who, heavily made up and dressed in sexy
Western clothes, sat outside bars at night or walked
about hand in hand with red-faced, beer-bellied
farangs. Nevertheless she had liked Nina, disliked
Sean and suspected him of being the real guilty party.

Offering to press Clary's skirt, she accompanied her
to her room on the first floor.

'I don't think it will need pressing, or only the
underskirt,' said Clary, as she rummaged in her
backpack for the clothes she had worn only a few
times since setting out from England.

Most of her garments were made of cotton, the only
comfortable material in countries where the climate
was hot and humid. But on the advice of an experienced woman traveller whose brains she had picked
before leaving London, she had included one ankle-
length full skirt of cream-spotted black polyester
georgette. Such a skirt, her adviser had told her, was
an invaluable standby for occasions—such as
tonight—when shorts or chinos wouldn't do.

'That is good,' Suthipong said approvingly, when
Clary shook out the skirt. 'Is there a blouse to match?'

'No, a top of this material would be hot and sticky.
I have this black cotton halter to go with it,' said Clary,
showing her the jersey-knit halter last worn at an unexpected party in Bali.

As she had small firm breasts she could go without
a bra without attracting amazed or disapproving
glances like the *farang* girls who showed their nipples
in clinging T-shirts or *farang* men who went about in
singlets or T-shirts with the sleeves ripped out.

'Why do Europeans walk about in their under-
wear?' a Thai had once asked her.

'Not all of them do,' she had answered, not for the first time embarrassed by the way some Europeans ignored the fact that the Thai were a very modest, neat and clean race who didn't like to see beach clothes on the streets of their cities.

At a quarter to seven, after first agreeing the fare with the driver, she climbed into one of the three-wheeled open-sided motor vehicles known as *tuk-tuks* from the noise they made.

As it moved off, she wondered if her arrival by this form of transport would cause raised eyebrows at a smart hotel. But when they got to the Mae Ping, a towering block with probably two hundred windows, most of them alight, in its slightly curving façade, a large sightseeing coach had just drawn up at the foot of the entrance steps. Nobody paid any attention to Clary as she climbed out and thanked her driver, receiving a friendly beam in response to her own smile.

A bell-boy opened the door for her and said, 'Good evening, *madame*,' as she entered the soaring lobby with its shining polished granite floor and lavish arrangements of orchids.

There was Thai music playing and, as she looked around for the reception desk and then walked towards it, she found that the music was live. It was being played by three musicians on a dais in a lounge leading off the lobby where two girls in long silk skirts, long-sleeved bodices and shoulder sashes were waiting to welcome people and take their orders for happy hour drinks.

At the moment Clary's bare shoulders were covered by a hand-painted silk scarf she had been unable to resist buying. Approaching the desk, she said to one

of the black-haired receptionists, 'Mr Lincoln is
expecting me. My name is Clarissa Hatfield.'

'Mr Lincoln is waiting for you, *madame*,' said the
Thai girl, with a gesture which made Clary turn
around.

Further on, beyond the reception and cashier's
desks, were some shops. She registered the glitter of
diamonds in a brightly lit window. On the other side
of the lobby from the desks which were now behind
her, a wide, thickly carpeted staircase led upwards.
Standing beside it, his arms folded across his broad
chest, was a very tall man, so tall that he dwarfed all
the Thais in the lobby and most of the foreigners as
well, including Clary.

As their eyes met, she had an intuitive feeling that
he had come down from the Executive Club to meet
her not solely out of curiosity but also to get a good
look at her before she saw him. He was looking her
up and down now, taking in every detail of her appearance with critical blue eyes under strongly marked
dark eyebrows.

As she looked back at him, she experienced a
strange sinking feeling and a strong desire to turn tail.
But now that she had announced herself there was no
way she could do that, and indeed no sensible reason
why she should be nervous of him. He was the kind
of personable stranger most women travelling alone
would be delighted to have cross their path.

Two strides and he was close enough to offer his
hand. 'Good evening. I'm Alistair Lincoln.' His
expression became slightly warmer, but he didn't
smile.

'Good evening.' She shook hands with him.

'We shall be dining in my suite,' he said. 'The reason for our meeting is better discussed in private, don't you think? Also I dislike being forced to listen to music not of my choosing, and I've already had to listen to an hour of it by the pool. It wouldn't surprise me if it's also piped to the restaurant. This way.'

Releasing her hand and transferring his to her elbow, he steered her in the direction of the lifts.

CHAPTER TWO

THE sitting-room of his suite could have been anywhere in the world except that there was a Thai
painting on the wall and the bases of the lamps at
either end of the sofa were gilded figures of Thai
dancers. But the furniture and built-in fitments, the
full-length curtains, the fitted carpet and silk lamp-
shades might have been in Los Angeles or London.

Clary's room at the Old Teak House had a floor
of polished teak planks, antique furniture including
the bed which was swathed in a mosquito net, and a
ceiling fan to stir the warm air.

She liked it much better than this room where the
artificial coolness of air-conditioning made her glad
of the scarf round her shoulders.

A waiter was putting finishing touches to a table
by the curtained window wall. He put his palms
together and gave Clary a smiling *wai*. 'Good evening,
madame.

She returned the smile but not the gesture. To *wai*
him would not have been correct.

'What would you like to drink?' Alistair Lincoln
asked her.

Clary had a half-bottle of a Thai whisky called
Mekhong—much cheaper than imported Scotch—in
her room. She drank it with Coke and ice at sundown.
Sometimes, reading in bed, she sipped another long
drink and then got up to brush her teeth and drink a
glass of water last thing.

Doubting that the well-stocked bar would include Mekhong, she said, 'A gin and tonic, please.'

'With ice and lemon, *madame*?' The waiter had left the table to come and serve their aperitifs.

'Yes, please.' She turned to her host. 'How was your flight? Are you feeling horribly jet-lagged?'

He didn't look it, she thought. He looked fresh and alert, a man of dynamic energy. Of course he had had several hours to rest and relax after the long flight from London, but she remembered feeling tired and lackadaisical for a couple of days after her arrival in the East. It was caused by the change of climate as much as by changing time zones.

'No, I've never experienced jet-lag—not even flying west, which is said to be the worst,' he answered. 'Years ago I was advised that the way to avoid it is not to eat anything but fruit, and not to drink anything but water. According to my adviser, the water tanks on aeroplanes are never completely cleaned out and there's a build-up of sludge, so it's better to stick to bottled water.'

It sounded a counsel of perfection which only an exceptionally self-disciplined person could stick to, thought Clary.

'But don't you get awfully bored without any meals or wine to help you pass the time? How long did it take you to get here?' she asked as, in response to his gesture, she seated herself in one of the comfortable armchairs on either side of the light wood coffee table.

'Ten and a half hours; a direct, non-stop flight over Russia and Afghanistan. Not such a long time to fill if one has a good book to read and some music of one's own choice. Do you like music, Miss Hatfield?'

'Very much. I have a Sanyo Sportser and half a dozen cassettes which I wouldn't be without for anything. I enjoy most kinds of music, but what I brought with me is mainly classical. I find it bears repetition better than pop.'

'I never listen to pop,' he said, with a dismissive shrug. 'Life is too short to waste one's time on rubbish.'

An opinionated man, she thought. Well, that was all right; she liked people who knew their own minds and had discriminating tastes and beliefs. As long as they weren't too dogmatic. Not *all* popular music was rubbish. But she hadn't come here to argue with him. She had come to unload her feeling of responsibility for Nina on to the broad shoulders under the well-cut coat of his lightweight suit.

She said, 'If your last meal was in London, you must be starving. Or were you here in time for lunch?'

'I had breakfast in the airport at Bangkok before flying on here. Then I had a light lunch by the pool. But this is my first drink since London.'

He must have signed to the waiter to fix two gin and tonics, and now they were ready and the waiter was placing hers in front of her, a paper mat under the tall glass and a plastic swizzle sticking out of the top of it.

When both drinks were in place, Alistair Lincoln thanked him and settled himself on the sofa at right angles to Clary's chair. His long-boned frame needed more space than the armchairs offered. It was just as well he could afford to fly first class, she thought.

Until she had learnt to request a seat by the emergency exit, she had always been uncomfortably cramped by the leg-room allowed between ordinary seats. For the man beside her, a long flight in tourist class would be unbearable. Yet the hand he stretched out for his glass was not the bunch of bananas that often went with a large frame. His fingers were lean and shapely. They looked capable of delicate, precise movements . . . gentle caresses.

Why that thought should enter her mind she couldn't imagine, and she didn't allow it to stay there for more than a second. Searching for something to say, but not wanting to mention Nina while the waiter was still in the room, she said, 'I flew out with Garuda, the Indonesian airline, and came to Chiang Mai on a bus. But I've heard Thai Airways is one of the world's best airlines. Would you agree with that?'

'They seem to be excellent,' he said. 'My favourite airline is Cathay Pacific.'

'Do you do a great deal of travelling?'

'Yes.' He left it at that, not explaining why or where.

Clary felt unfairly snubbed. It was difficult to make conversation with a stranger without asking some questions. She hadn't intended to pry. She reached for her drink and lifted it to her lips. Most people said 'cheers' or 'skol' or something friendly before tasting their first drink with someone else. But Alistair Lincoln had already swallowed a slug of his without observing that convention, so she saw no reason to wish him good health or happy days before sipping hers.

Having arranged the dining table to his satisfaction, the waiter bowed and departed, presumably to return at some appointed time with the first course.

When he had left the room, Clary was suddenly aware that being alone with a stranger in a secluded place was one of the situations women were advised to avoid. But the reason Alistair Lincoln had given for bringing her up here had seemed a reasonable one, and he didn't look the kind of man whose sex life, or lack of it, impelled him to make unwelcome passes. For all she knew he might be married now, but in that case surely he would have brought his wife with him.

'You described yourself as a backpacker, Miss Hatfield. I must say your present appearance is considerably at variance with that of the average backpacker. A scruffy lot, in my observation. Unwashed hair... grubby jeans... smelly trainers or sneakers.'

'I think that's unfair, Mr Lincoln. It's not always easy to keep oneself neat and clean when one's travelling around on buses and staying at the cheapest places. But most travellers do their best, and often their manners and their respect for local customs are superior to the behaviour of other, better-off tourists. I've never seen a backpacker sitting on a Buddha to be photographed like the American fashion model who was fined for sacrilege recently. You'd think she, and a team from a top French fashion magazine, would have known better, wouldn't you?'

'I should indeed,' he agreed. 'How much was the fine?'

'Three thousand *baht*, which is just under seventy pounds, so really quite lenient. The police seized five rolls of film and at first the model and photographer were each sentenced to three years' imprisonment plus a heavier fine. But after they pleaded guilty the fine was halved and the prison sentence suspended.'

'Nina's plea was not guilty, I presume?'

'Yes, and I'm quite sure she's not . . . or only in the sense of being an unwilling accessory to someone else's offence.'

He crossed his long legs. Like his hands, his feet were not huge, and he was elegantly shod in highly polished black loafers over pale grey silk socks.

'You'd better tell me everything you know from the beginning,' he said. 'On the telephone yesterday you said you weren't a friend of Nina's, merely lodging at the same guesthouse. How often have you seen her?'

'I spent both the morning and afternoon visiting hours with her last Friday, and another hour yesterday morning.'

'On the strength of three hours in her company, I doubt if you are as good a judge of her character as I am, Miss Hatfield . . . or may I call you Clarissa?'

'Yes, if you wish . . . but I'm usually known as Clary.'

'Do you prefer that name?'

She nodded. 'Much! I hate Clarissa. There are people it might suit, but I'm not one of them. I would rather have been Jane or Mary or . . .' She broke off, conscious that he couldn't be in the least interested in her feelings about her Christian name. Reverting to the previous subject, she said, 'As for being a judge of Nina's character, I don't claim to be. I only know that it isn't right for a girl of her age to be in her situation without anyone to help her. And it may be that she has changed since you last saw her, Mr Lincoln . . . Alistair,' she amended. 'I understand that was about five years ago.'

He nodded, his expression darkening, making him look for a moment a very hard man indeed.

'I hope she has, but her present predicament doesn't suggest much improvement. She was spoilt from birth,' he said coldly.

'She's certainly not being spoilt at the moment,' Clary replied drily. 'And if she's been spoilt in the past, prison must be a thousand times worse for her than for someone accustomed to hardships. Quite apart from the physical privations, there's the horrible feeling of betrayal... of being left to carry the can by the person who really bought the pot.'

'Who *allegedly* bought the pot,' he corrected her.

The remark caused Clary to wonder if he might be a high-powered lawyer, a barrister earning colossal fees by taking part in those trials which went on for weeks and cost hundreds of thousands of pounds. But she had the impression that such men were usually forty or more before they became high earners and, from what his stepsister had told her, Alistair had already been rich five years ago.

'Who, according to Nina, was that person?' he asked.

Clary told him about Sean, omitting to mention, at this stage, that Sean and Nina had been lovers. She didn't want to say anything which would lower his already low opinion of the girl until he had seen for himself the miserable conditions she was living in.

By the time she had given him a slightly abridged account of the facts as far as she knew them, they had finished their drinks and the waiter had returned, wheeling in a trolley with the sides of a pale pink damask cloth folded over whatever was on it and accompanied by a second waiter.

'I hope you don't mind, I chose our meal in advance, but if I've ordered anything you particularly dislike it can easily be changed,' said Alistair, as they moved to the dining table where the waiters had drawn out the chairs for them.

'I'm sure that won't be necessary,' said Clary, as she sat down. 'There are very few things I dislike, although I've learnt to be careful of some of the sauces served with Thai food.' She glanced up at the waiter, who was unfolding a starched linen napkin for her. 'I like Thai food very much, but the peppers called *phrik kii noo* are like fire in the mouth,' she said, smiling.

He smiled back. 'Thank you, *madame*. I am glad you enjoy our Thai food but, as you say, mouse shit peppers are very hot...too hot for many visitors.' With a practised gesture he spread the napkin on her lap.

'Thank you.' Her face expressionless, she flicked a swift glance at Alistair.

Their eyes met and for an instant his blue ones, previously cold, were suddenly lit by a gleam of the same amusement she was suppressing.

After the waiters had served the first course and withdrawn, he said, 'I wonder where he picked up that particular idiom?'

'From a mischievous *farang*, presumably. If there's ever an opportune moment, it might be a kindness to tell him there are more polite translations of *phrik kii noo*.'

'Have you picked up much Thai?'

'Hardly any. It's a difficult language for Westerners because the words change their meaning according to the tone they're spoken in, and we don't use tones in that way. I've learnt enough to be polite and to haggle in the markets, but that's as far as I've got. Are you a linguist?'

'I speak Spanish and French and some German. Let's have the curtains open, shall we?'

He rose to pull them apart, using the concealed draw-cords and revealing a panoramic view of Chiang Mai by night, some of its many temples floodlit but not so brightly as a sports stadium on the university side of the city.

'You can't see it clearly now, but over there is a mountain called Doi Suthep which the porter who brought up my baggage said I should visit,' said Alistair. 'Have you been up there?'

'Not yet. It's best to go up on a clear day, and the weather has been rather hazy since I've been here. I may have to skip Doi Suthep. It's time I was moving on. I should have left here on Monday if it hadn't been for Nina. But I couldn't leave town without doing something to help her. Now you're here she doesn't need me. I'll see her on Friday to say goodbye and then I'll be on my way.'

'Where are you going next?'

'To Koh Samui, an island in the Gulf of Thailand.' On impulse, she added, 'I have a thing about islands. The first one I went to was Bali, which was wonderful, and the last was Penang in Malaysia.'

Not wishing to bore him with too much talk about herself, she changed the subject, saying, 'These prawns are delicious.'

The peeled prawns were nestling in a hot cheese sauce, accompanied by rolls, also hot, and butter.

'Yes, they're good,' he agreed. 'But the cuisine here is adapted to foreigners' tastes. Tomorrow I'd like to try some authentic Thai cooking. Can you recommend somewhere?'

'For that you would have to forgo all these elegant trappings,' she said, indicating the ice bucket, the candles encircled by orchids, the polished bronze cutlery and cut crystal glasses. 'I think the most authentic Thai cooking comes in pretty basic surroundings such as the food stalls near the night market. I've eaten there several times, but then I'm not used to all this.'

'You look as if you are,' he answered. 'What were you doing before you set out on your travels?'

Remembering his monosyllabic reply to her question about *his* travels, she said evasively, 'Nothing exciting . . . nothing I want to go back to.'

She touched her napkin to her lips and turned to look at the view, wondering if he would press her for a more explicit answer.

He didn't. Instead he began to question her about Nina's trial and whether his stepsister had been represented by a lawyer.

'I don't know too much about it,' Clary admitted. 'I think Nina was in shock throughout the court proceedings. I don't think she took much in. What surprises me is that, if the case was reported in the *Bangkok Post* or *The Nation*, as I'm sure it must have been, it wasn't picked up by the news agencies and then by the papers in England, where you would have seen it.'

'They may have used it,' he said. 'But that sort of story gets more space in the tabloids than in the serious Press, and anyway I haven't time to read more than the front-page news and the leader page.'

The waiters came back to remove the first course and serve the second: two pineapples cut so they would lie on their sides, the upper side forming a lid which,

removed, showed the fruit had been hollowed out and
refilled with a mixture of chicken, pineapple and rice.

When the waiters had gone, Alistair said, 'I've arranged for a first-class interpreter to come here early
tomorrow and help me to sort things out. That may
be achieved quite quickly, or it may take some time.
You said on the telephone that Nina had lost touch
with her mother. How did that happen?'

'When Nina last heard from her, her mother was
going on a cruise on a private yacht for some months.
Nina has some of the details, but not enough to cable
her mother for help.'

'Which she might not get if she could,' he said sardonically. 'Nina's mother lives on her looks and her
wits . . . which won't be getting easier now that she's
in her forties. If she has a fat fish on her line, she'll
be concentrating on landing him and nothing else will
matter to her, least of all her daughter. Is Nina pretty?'

'I should think when she's well and happy, she must
be extremely pretty. At the moment she's run down
and scared, but even so—yes, she's pretty.'

Alistair reached for the bottle of white wine in the
ice bucket to replenish their glasses.

'A pretty daughter is an encumbrance to a woman
like Aileen. If she knew where Nina was, she would
probably be pleased to have her safely out of the way
for some years,' he said cynically.

While he dealt with the wine, Clary had been
looking out of the window, ostensibly at the lights:
street lamps, the headlights and brake lights of cars,
a few neon signs. Actually she had been studying
Alistair's reflection in the glass, noting the way his
dark hair—almost as black as Thai hair—grew from

his forehead and temples, and the commanding lines of his nose, slanted cheekbones and jaw.

Not a face one would easily forget, once having seen it; and all the more striking in Thailand, where every third girl was a beauty but good-looking men were harder to find. Many Thai men had pleasant faces, but the bones were more softly moulded than the forceful structure underlying the taut skin of the man mirrored in the window.

The contemptuous bite of his reference to Nina's mother made Clary turn to look at him. 'I can't believe any woman would be glad to have her daughter in jail.'

'Can't you?' He gave a slight shrug. 'Perhaps you're an idealist who prefers to see only the best in human nature and ignore the unpleasant aspects. I'm a realist. I see people the way they are...good, bad or indifferent. Nina's mother is a selfish opportunist, and it's more than likely her daughter will turn out exactly like her.'

'Then why are you here?' said Clary. 'If you feel that way about them, why did you come?'

CHAPTER THREE

ALISTAIR drank some wine before he answered.

Finally he said, 'Two reasons. It was raining when you rang up. It had been raining for days. I thought some time in the sun would make an agreeable change. Also I wanted to see if your face matched your voice. As no doubt you've often been told, you have a very beautiful voice.'

Clary was momentarily dumbfounded. Of course he couldn't be serious. No man flew halfway round the world because the weather was wet and he was curious about the stranger who had rung him up.

Torn by conflicting reactions, she answered, with some asperity, 'I hope you aren't next going to humbug me that it does.'

Her tart riposte seemed to amuse him. 'Be grateful you aren't a beauty,' he told her blandly. 'A friend of mine is a cosmetic surgeon who spends his days taking tucks in the faces of women frantic at losing their looks. Your voice and the way you walk are more durable assets. I watched you come into the lobby and was struck by how gracefully you moved—partly, of course, because you're wearing low heels, not three-inch stilettos.'

'I'm too tall already,' said Clary, feeling a glow of unwilling pleasure at these unaccustomed compliments.

'Not for a man of my height.'

The glint in his eyes made her drop her glance. He was flirting with her. She didn't wish to be flirted with, especially not here, *à deux* in his luxurious sitting-room with an equally luxurious bedroom only a few steps away.

Did he think that, after he had wined and dined her, she would allow him to coax her into the bedroom?

Since her arrival in Thailand, Clary's already disenchanted view of men had become even more disillusioned. Although travellers she had met in other parts of south-east Asia had warned her to avoid Pattaya, a seaside resort not far from Bangkok which had become notorious as a sink of every vice, the sad sight of young Thai girls in the company of much older Western men, with whom they were unable to exchange more than a few words, was commonplace everywhere. Some of the girls, she had heard, had been sold into prostitution. She felt pity for them and disgust for their patrons.

Consequently the possibility that the man on the other side of the table might be expecting to have her for dessert made her angry and uneasy. Part of her was flattered by his praise of her voice and her grace, but the feminist in her resented his assumption that, at this early stage of their acquaintance, his compliments would be acceptable.

To depersonalise the conversation, she said in a matter-of-fact tone, 'I think being very tall is only a problem when one is growing up and going through the self-conscious stage. After that it's not a serious inconvenience. In fact some of my average-sized friends complain that people of my size have a better deal, clothes-wise, than they do, a lot of ready-to-wear skirts and trousers being too long for them. Do you find it difficult to get clothes which fit?'

He shook his head. 'No, because I have my suits made and buy jeans in America where there are a lot of tall people. I find my height an advantage; except in low-beamed country pubs and small cars...and single beds.'

Until he added this rider, Clary had felt that the conversation was coming back on to safe ground. But now, even though her eyes were on the food on her plate, she knew that his were on her. Every instinct told her that he wasn't thinking about single beds but about the double bed in the next room and having her in it with him.

And mixed with her resentment of his lustful thoughts about her—for there was no doubt in her mind that in *his* mind she was already naked and pliant in his arms—was an involuntary tremor of excitement and curiosity at what it might be like to spend the night with him. It had been so long since a man had held her and kissed her. More than a year. A long time to live alone, sleep alone. Especially for someone accustomed to a loving relationship...or rather what she had thought was a loving relationship.

Picking up her wine glass, she said, 'This French wine is very good, but it may be that in a few years the Thais won't have to import so much wine. A Frenchman who runs a restaurant here tells me that since they began their own viniculture a few years ago they've made great strides. I tried a Thai wine at his place which, if not as good as this, was very drinkable and of course much less expensive.'

'They also grow strawberries in this part of Thailand, I gather.'

She nodded. 'I've seen great mounds of wonderful-looking strawberries on street stalls, but I haven't bought any. I usually stick to fruits I can peel. How did you know about the strawberries?'

'I was told about them when I was choosing dinner. We're having a strawberry pudding. I'd expect any fruit used here to be properly washed, wouldn't you?'

'Yes, I'm sure it is,' she agreed, relieved that he was no longer looking at her with that disturbing glint in his eyes.

His irises were the colour of a length of Thai silk she had seen but had thought too vivid a blue for her mother. Bette Hatfield liked soft colours, rose pink and baby blue.

'You can't see it from where you're sitting, but a few yards from this hotel there's a group of shacks,' he went on. 'I always travel with a small pair of fieldglasses, mainly for looking at birds. This afternoon I had a close look at the shacks and their occupants. God knows how they manage it, but the people down there are clean, and I saw one youth coming out whose shirt and trousers were immaculate. Yet they don't seem to have any water or drainage, and this evening, at dusk, food was being cooked on a camp fire. There were similar plumes of smoke rising all over the city.'

This turn in the conversation made Clary much more relaxed. As she told him how, in the morning, he would probably be able to watch saffron-robed Buddhist monks going about the streets with their alms bowls, she was also reminding herself that it was the nature of men to correlate women and sex, even when they had no intention of doing anything about it. Wasn't it better for him to look at a woman of his own race and age-group, and contemplate bedding her, than to pay for the services, possibly under duress, of some fragile little creature half his size and half his age?

The strawberry pudding was a mousse decorated with whole fruit and whipped cream. Clary was amused to notice the schoolboyish relish with which Alistair ate his.

It was followed by coffee and liqueurs, but she declined the latter. Presently, after a glance at her watch, she said, 'I'd like to get back to the guesthouse by ten, if you don't mind. I go to bed early and get up at first light to enjoy the cool time before sunrise. I expect this hotel shows English-language movies on the video channel of the TV. A couple I met, who were staying at a big place like this, told me the ten o'clock movie was a godsend while they were adjusting from European time to Thai time.'

He checked the time by his own watch. It wasn't, she noticed, a Rolex Oyster or any of the status-symbol watches. She knew most of them by sight now because there were stalls selling cheap copies of costly watches all along the street, not far from here, which was the centre of the night market.

But she hadn't seen a copy of the plain steel-braceleted watch on the sinewy wrist, lightly covered with dark hair, revealed when Alistair pushed back his cuff. Perhaps he didn't care for expensive adornments of that sort. He wore no ring and his shirt cuff was held by a pearl button, not a gold or jewelled cuff-link.

'Still early afternoon in England,' he said. 'What I'd prefer to a movie is to stretch my legs. Is it far to the guesthouse? Could I walk you home?'

'Yes, by all means...but I think you'll be hot in a jacket...even in a long-sleeved shirt. Have you a sports shirt with you?'

He nodded. 'I'll go and change. Excuse me.'

Perversely, now that the danger of having a pass made at her seemed to be over, Clary was conscious of...what? Disappointment? No. Puzzlement. Why had he backed off?

Because he had read the signs that she wasn't a one-night-stand girl? Because he had changed his mind and decided he wasn't interested? Because he had only been trying it on without any serious intention of following through, not being a one-night-stand man?

She found herself hoping the third explanation was the correct one. Though really the only thing about him which mattered to her was that he was willing and able to get Nina out of prison.

He came back wearing the same trousers with a lemon-yellow linen sports shirt. Clary had noticed that the Thais looked their best in colours such as coral, orange, lime green and yellow. Black and drab colours didn't suit them. Similarly Alistair, with his dark hair and olive skin, looked good in the lemon shirt which, curiously, emphasised the blueness of his eyes more than a blue shirt would have done.

His forearms were neither pale nor soft like the arms of many European men. Still retaining a trace of tan from some previous trip to the sun, they were the muscular arms of a man who, even if he were not obliged to exert himself physically, chose to keep himself strong and fit.

They had second cups of coffee and then went down to the lobby.

'Taxi, sir?' asked one of the doormen.

'No, thanks ... we're walking.'

Clary was glad to be back in the natural temperature of the tropical night. If, after a year in the East,
she were forced to make a choice between a climate
which was sometimes too hot and one which could
be uncomfortably cold, she would choose the heat.

'What's that?' asked Alistair.

He was looking at a structure beside the hotel's
driveway which bore some resemblance to a large and
ornate bird house, lit up and hung with garlands of
jasmine.

'That's the hotel's spirit house. All buildings in
Thailand have them.'

'Where you go?' The question came from one of
the *tuk-tuk* drivers waiting for fares in the street
outside the hotel.

'Walking,' said Alistair.

She was pleased to notice that he smiled at the man
and didn't ignore him as some tourists did when ac-
costed. But that was usually a sign of being nervous
in a strange environment. She couldn't imagine any
situation in which the tall man beside her would be
nervous.

When she had first come to Chiang Mai, a city of
a hundred thousand inhabitants, other girls staying
at the guesthouse had told her it was safe to walk
about alone at night, providing one used common
sense and avoided dark alleys. Nevertheless it was
nicer to have a longer shadow next to her shadow as
they passed the street lamps.

'Look how the decoration on that temple glitters
in the headlights of passing cars.' They were walking
along the outer bank of the moat when she drew his

attention to a *wat* on the inner side of the waterway. 'Isn't it beautiful?'

Alistair murmured agreement. He sounded preoccupied and he must have been thinking about his stepsister, because a moment later he said, 'Has anyone tried to sell you pot while you've been here?'

'No, never—but probably I don't look a likely customer...older than a lot of backpackers...more conventionally dressed. And I don't smoke cigarettes, so it isn't very likely I'd smoke pot. The sellers must size up potential customers before they make an approach, don't you think?'

'I guess so.' For the first time he seemed to notice that after leaving the hotel she had removed the scarf and now was bare-shouldered except for the strap of the halter.

He said, 'Were you cold during dinner? I'm sorry: I should have realised the air-con might be too low for someone used to this heat. Thoughtless of me. I assumed the silk thing round your shoulders was worn for effect, not warmth.'

'Don't worry: I expected it to be cool inside the hotel. If I'd been really cold I'd have told you.'

'I hope so. What's the mosquito situation here? Do you use a repellent at night? You're exposing a fair bit of skin and your legs are bare too, I presume?'

'We have nets on the beds at the guesthouse, but I haven't been bitten in Chiang Mai and I haven't used anti-mozz stuff. I did when I went on a trek to two hill tribe villages.'

'Was that an interesting experience?'

'Not as interesting as five years ago when not many people were trekking. I'd heard that some of the villages were becoming like human zoos, so I shopped

around for a trek to a more remote place. But even
there the first signs of commercialisation were visible.
If all the hill tribe embroidery on sale in Chiang Mai
were the genuine article, the hill women would have
to be sewing non-stop for twenty-four hours a day!
Obviously most of the stuff is as fake as the Vuitton
luggage and the Chanel belts.'

They had left the main streets behind them and were
now in a quiet *soi* overhung by the branches of trees
in the private gardens on either side.

'That's a pity but inevitable, I suppose,' said
Alistair. 'The world no longer has room for primitive
people untouched by civilisation. There's hardly a
place on the globe out of reach of tourism. Like you,
I'd have liked to see Thailand when it was Siam. But
from what I've read, travelling in the East was quite
a hazardous exercise in the days of quinine and pith
helmets.'

The *soi* was crossed by another. As she turned to
the left, Clary said, 'I hope you have a good sense of
direction and don't get lost on your way back. If you
do, all the *tuk-tuk* drivers know where the Mae Ping
is. I don't use the bicycle *samlors* at night because
they don't have lights.'

'Don't worry: I shan't get lost,' he said, sounding
rather amused. 'What about tomorrow? I'll be busy
all morning, but let's meet for lunch and I'll tell you
what progress I've made . . . if any,' he added drily.

'All right, but let's eat at Daret's . . . my treat,' Clary
suggested. 'It's a place where travellers go as opposed
to tourists.'

He might raise his eyebrows at the tablecloths at
Daret's, and the way that the waiters wore feather
dusters, hooked like tails to the backs of their trousers,

with which to flick off the crumbs between customers. Also, compared with the Mae Ping, the prices were ludicrously cheap there. But even though the bill would be a fraction of what tonight's meal would cost him, she wanted to make it clear that she wasn't a freeloader.

'I have a better idea. Let's take a picnic up to the temple on the mountain. After a morning grappling with Thai bureaucracy, I shall probably be in need of spiritual refreshment.'

They had come to the gate of the guesthouse.

'Yes, I think you may,' she agreed. 'From what I've heard, dealing with Thais can be quite tricky for Europeans. The Thais *never* blow their tops and people who do lose face. Not that I would expect you to get in a temper, but you might say something critical, and that's unacceptable too.'

'The only person I'm likely to lose my cool with is Nina,' was Alistair's somewhat clipped reply.

'So that's settled,' he went on. 'I'll get the hotel to put up a packed lunch for us, and lay on a car, and I'll be here as soon after one as I can make it. Until tomorrow, then. Goodnight, Clary.'

And before she could question any of these arrangements, he was gone, striding away down the moonlit *soi* with the athletic lope of a man whose tall frame was built of strong bones clad with powerful muscles and a minimum of flesh.

Later, lying inside the diaphanous tent of mosquito netting, with her door open on to the balcony which went all the way round the first floor, Clary thought over the evening.

She had wondered if going to Mae Ping for dinner might make her dissatisfied with the way she was seeing the world and hanker for the fleshpots. But it hadn't.

As she and Alistair were leaving the hotel, some people had been arriving with a large set of matched suitcases obviously filled with fashionable resort clothes and all the accessories necessary for a de luxe winter break. She could honestly say that she hadn't felt a twinge of envy for them, or for any of the other fat cats staying at the Mae Ping.

Not that 'fat cat' was an apt description for the lean and self-disciplined man with whom she had just spent the evening, she thought, smiling to herself.

Neither, it seemed, was 'wolf', although there had been a stage when she'd thought that it might be.

Just what kind of man *was* he? After three hours in his company she didn't know much more about him than when they had first shaken hands.

But then I didn't really know Miles, and I lived with him for three years ... believed we would spend the rest of our lives together, were her next thoughts.

I didn't even know myself. Somehow I convinced myself that I was happy and fulfilled, living life in the fast lane, as Miles called it. Perhaps I was for a while. But all the time, deep down inside, there was this other self ... the slow-lane person I am now.

Turning on her side, her few valuables—passport, credit card, travellers' cheques—tucked safely inside the pillowcase, she closed her eyes and went to sleep.

When Alistair had said he would lay on transport to Doi Suthep, Clary had thought it would be a drive-yourself car, not a Mercedes with a chauffeur at the wheel.

Fortunately everyone staying at the guesthouse had gone out for the day, and only Suthipong and her mother saw the gleaming limousine arrive and depart with Clary and her small shopping knapsack in the back.

'What have you got in there?' Alistair asked, as the Mercedes moved off.

'I thought the hotel's packed lunch might be a bit dull, so I bought a few local snacks for you to try,' she explained. Eager to hear his news, she said, 'How did it go? Have you made any headway?'

'I don't think there'll be any difficulty about getting Nina out . . . if I'm prepared to pay the exorbitant fine imposed on her.' He gave her a sardonic look. 'You didn't tell me about that.'

'It seemed possible that, once you were here, they might adjust the fine to get her off their hands,' she answered. 'After all, it costs them something, if not much, to keep *farangs* in jail . . . and a lot of prices in Thailand are negotiable. You do give the impression of being quite well off,' she added, indicating the car they were sitting in and the uniformed driver.

Alistair made no reply to that. He was wearing the suit he had worn last night but had taken off the coat and tossed it over the back of the front passenger seat. Now he took off his striped tie and opened the collar of his shirt before starting to roll up the sleeves.

'We're going to stop at the zoo and have lunch there. I'm told there's an excellent aviary which I'd like to see before we go up the mountain. I hope birds don't bore you.'

'No, I like them . . . animals too.'

Less than half an hour later they were sitting on a shaded bench in the park-like grounds of Chiang Mai zoo.

'This is a very grand picnic,' said Clary, who hadn't expected her lunch to be set out on a folding table with plates and cutlery from a fitted wicker hamper brought to the spot by the driver, table under one arm, hamper on the other shoulder. There was also a cool box containing water and wine which Alistair had carried.

Faced with all this elegance—linen napkins, tiny pots of caviar on ice for starters—she hardly liked to unpack her own contributions, all bought from street stalls and parcelled in bags and cones made from the pages of out-of-date Thai magazines.

The chauffeur had gone off to have his lunch in the zoo's cafeteria. Filling two tumblers with water, Alistair said, 'Having hired one of the hotel's cars and a driver to give myself maximum "face" for this morning's meetings, I thought it seemed logical to keep it for the afternoon expedition. Otherwise I should have picked you up in a taxi.'

He took a long drink of water, before asking, 'Is the Mercedes an embarrassment to you? Do you see it as a symbol of capitalist decadence...or élitism...or whatever jargon the grudgers are currently using to proclaim their belief that no one should have anything which everyone else hasn't got?'

His tone had a sharp edge of sarcasm, but Clary remained unflustered. 'Not at all,' she said calmly. 'I'm just rather amused by the contrast between your provisions and mine. Look...'

She unfastened her knapsack, took out a package covered with Thai writing and opened it to display the bite-sized coconut cakes she had watched being shaped and cooked in the food market that morning.

Alistair put one in his mouth. 'They're good,' he said, chewing. Then: 'Sorry if I snapped at you. It's been a trying morning. I dislike being involved in this situation, and having to keep an ingratiating smile on my face went much against the grain.'

'Yes, it must have been very difficult,' she said sympathetically. 'Let's talk about it later, not while we're having lunch. Tell me about your interest in birds? How did that start?'

'It began with a pair of binoculars I bought for five pounds from a junk shop near my boarding school...'

As he talked, she formed the impression that he had been rather a loner, a boy who preferred wandering off on his own to going around in a group or with one or two close companions.

After lunch, when the driver had returned, they left him repacking the hamper and walked round the zoo, where birds and animals were housed in large naturalistic cages and enclosures.

The birds which appealed most to Clary were the pheasants; a Great Argus pheasant with an immense spotted tail, a Crested Fireback with a blue mask, dark steel blue plumage, a bronze back and white tail and—perhaps the most beautiful of all—a Silver Pheasant with black speckles on mainly white plumage, pink legs and a cardinal-red mask.

The birds of prey, eagles and hawks, were less colourful creatures, and while Alistair studied them, she watched him and wondered about him. She had learned a little bit more during lunch, but not very much; not as much as she wanted to know.

I'm attracted to him, she thought. I should have left here today…said goodbye to Nina by letter. After I've seen her tomorrow, I must leave Chiang Mai without fail. Hanging about, seeing more of him, can only lead to trouble.

In the car going up to the temple behind a *songthaew*, one of the small pick-up trucks with a bench along each side, Clary saw the Thai passengers give a respectful *wai* on passing a wayside shrine. Then the Mercedes overtook the *songthaew* and sped up the steep winding road bordered by tall trees and jungle.

Where the road widened out below the temple, the driver parked the car near the lifts.

'I'd rather walk up the Stairway to Heaven,' said Clary. 'I'll meet you at the top.' She turned away in the direction of the long staircase crowded with Thais and foreigners going up and coming down.

'We'll both go the hard way,' said Alistair. 'How many steps? Do you know?'

'About three hundred, I think.'

The balustrades on either side of the staircase were *nagas*, dragon-headed serpents, with long undulating bodies clad with ceramic-scales. At the bottom of the steps a woman was selling small birds in wicker containers shaped like Cornish pasties.

'Poor little devils.' Alistair frowned at the restless flutter of wings unable to spread.

'They're not being sold to be kept in captivity,' Clary explained. 'People buy them and release them to "make merit".'

'Trapping and caging the birds is not earning any demerits as long as it makes merit for others and money for the vendors, I suppose? There seems to be a good deal of double-think in this culture,' Alistair said caustically.

'That's true of *all* cultures, don't you think?' Clary set off up the steps.

It would have not been much of a climb in a temperate climate, but the sun was still burning fiercely and there were beads of sweat sliding between her shoulder blades when she reached the outer courtyard of the fourteenth-century *wat*.

Nuns, dressed in white robes with their hair cut mannishly short, were selling lotus buds for Buddhist visitors to offer at the shrines. Foreigners wearing shorts were being handed loose cotton trousers to cover their legs inside the temple, and everyone who wanted to go in had to remove their shoes and leave them on racks by the door.

The temple was several thousand feet above sea-level. A refreshingly cool breeze was blowing through the cloisters as they walked round looking at the many golden images of the Lord Buddha seated in the lotus position, apparently lost in meditation.

Clary wondered if the calm of the temple was soothing her companion's irritation at the events of the morning and, more recently, at the caging of small wild birds.

She couldn't believe that, having come all this way, he wouldn't rescue his stepsister, however much it cost him. Equally she couldn't see him being kind and supportive to Nina after he had got her out.

'Would you like an ice-cream?' she asked, as they returned to the outer courtyard.

'Would you?'

'I'll get them,' she said firmly. 'You go and find a seat with a view of the city.' She waved him off in the direction of Chiang Mai while she went the other way to the café.

He was leaning on a balustrade, looking down at the plain, when she joined him, holding two cornets.

'How old are you, Clary?' he asked, watching her lick her ice.

'Twenty-seven. How old are you?'

'Thirty-six. Last night I put you at twenty-three or four. Today, with no make-up and your hair blowing about, you look about Nina's age.'

'I'm glad I'm not. At nineteen I wasn't at all "together". Now I think I'm on the right track...that I'm really beginning to know what life's all about.'

'Which is?'

'To be true to oneself...sounds easy enough but isn't.'

He received that in silence. She wondered what he was thinking. A clangour broke out behind them. Looking over their shoulders, they saw several Thais bending to swing the clappers of a line of enormous bells.

When the booming had died away, Clary said, 'What is your guiding principle?'

'Not dissimilar to yours. To define what one wants and go for it.'

It sounded to her quite different from her philosophy. 'Go for it' had an aggressive, acquisitive ring.

Alistair finished his ice and, turning his back on the view, leaned against the stone parapet with his arms folded over his chest as they had been when she had first seen him.

He said, 'You must tell me how much I owe you for that long-distance call. There's no reason why you should be out of pocket on Nina's account.'

She shook her head. 'It didn't cost that much. Forget it. I was glad to do it.'

After a pause, he said, 'How far would you go to help Nina?'

Rather at a loss, she answered, 'I'd do whatever I could ... but now that you're here she doesn't need help from me.'

'On the contrary, you're her lifeline. What happens to her depends entirely on you.'

'I don't understand ...'

Alistair looked down at her and suddenly in the blue eyes she saw the amorous gleam of the night before.

'I'll get Nina out of jail ... if you will agree to spend two weeks——'

He broke off with a frown as the sonorous booming of the bells began again.

Clary looked at him, aghast. Could she be as mistaken about this man as she had been about Miles?

Was it possible that standing beside her was a womaniser so unscrupulous that he would go to any lengths to get a girl he wanted; even to the extent of threatening not to pay Nina's fine if Clary wouldn't consent to his outrageous proposition?

CHAPTER FOUR

ALL the bells in the courtyard seemed to be ringing in concert as a large party of Thais, adults and children, scurried about shaking every clapper they could find. It was impossible to speak while the din continued. With the wind in the right direction, the bells might even be audible in Chiang Mai down on the plain.

As Alistair waited for the sound to abate, his scowl of annoyance gave place to resigned amusement at the way he had been interrupted in midproposition. A shrug indicated that he would continue when he could hear himself speak.

Clary, too, was forced to contain her feelings. As she waited impatiently for the clanging to subside, indignation fizzed round her brain like the lighted fuse once used to set off explosives.

All the anger and pain she had felt but never expressed when Miles let her down came bubbling up from some place deep in her being. She discovered that she hadn't purged it, merely suppressed it. It was still there, as bitter as bile, and it couldn't be contained any longer.

This time she would let it all out: tell this arrogant bastard what she thought of him and all the men like him—and God knew there were plenty of them. Nina's ex-boyfriend Sean, for example. Not to mention all the sexist beasts who paraded their poor little slave-girls in public as if renting a girl was no worse than renting a car.

I hate you! I hate the lot of you, Clary thought fiercely. There may be a few exceptions but, when you get down to brass tacks, men as a species are one big pain in the 'a'. They've messed up running the world. They have egos as big as watermelons. Half of them can't find their socks without a woman to help them. And the biggest irony of all is that, though *they* all enjoy sex, if they're mostly like Miles—and I bet they are—they don't make it all that wonderful for their partners.

Aloud, raising her voice to be heard above the subsiding ding-dongs, she said in her most cutting tone, 'I wouldn't spend two weeks with you if you offered me a suite at the Oriental, sapphires for breakfast and rubies for tea, Mr Lincoln. As for being coerced by that subtle threat not to help Nina . . . forget it. I don't believe even you would be such a rat as to leave her to rot in jail. But if you do, believe me, I'll find some way to get her out and to show you in your true colours . . . if it's the last thing I do. I'm going back to Chiang Mai—on the bus! I hope we *don't* meet again!'

Trembling with anger, she marched off, heading for the Stairway to Heaven.

She had only gone a few yards when a powerful hand fell on her shoulder, forcing her to a standstill.

'Now just hang on a minute . . .'

'Let me go. *Take your hand off me!*' Far too angry to care about *jai yen*, the cool heart admired by the Thais, she allowed her temper to show in her sparkling eyes and furious voice.

Alistair ignored her demand. 'Listen to me, will you, please?' But in spite of the 'please' it was an order, not a request.

'No, I will not. Oh . . . get lost!'

Aware of the curious stares they were beginning to attract, Clary struck off his hand by means of a vigorous blow with the edge of her hand against his forearm. Then, not putting it past him to use his superior strength to grab her and make her stand still, she began to run to the stairs.

'Clary . . . don't be a fool! Come back here!'

Now that the bells were silent, the commanding English voice rang out across the courtyard, causing all heads to turn. Even more furious with him for making her the cynosure of many pairs of surprised and disapproving dark eyes, Clary reached the top of the steps and began to hurry down them, dodging her way between the people coming up and those descending.

The staircase was straight, built in a series of flights with landings between them. Even so it looked a very long way down and unpleasantly steep and dizzy-making to anyone who, like Clary, suffered from vertigo in high places.

In her right mind she would never have tried to rush down nearly four hundred steps. But she was deeply upset, not just by Alistair's insulting suggestion but by memories from the past. The thought of having a public row with him all the way down the staircase, and perhaps—ultimate humiliation—bursting into tears, made her continue her impetuous descent, striving to keep her eyes on the flight she was on and not see the others below it.

All might have been well had her hurrying feet not made contact with something dropped on the steps. She never saw what she slipped on. It could have been a fruit, a squashy cake or even the spot on which someone had spat. Her left foot skidded, throwing her whole body off balance. She tried to recover herself but couldn't and fell, tumbling down four or five steps to the next landing and, on the way, banging her head against the serpent balustrade.

Slightly stunned by the quite hard blow to the side of her skull, she lay in an ungainly heap, wanting to pick herself up but feeling dazed and confused. People began to cluster round her, everyone talking at once and adding to her confusion and embarrassment.

And then as several pairs of hands were starting to help her to her feet, an authoritative voice said, 'No! Leave her,' and the tone, if not the words, were understood and the crowd round her suddenly drew back and left Alistair looming over her.

He didn't loom long but swiftly crouched down beside her. 'Don't move. You may have broken something.'

'I haven't . . . I'm fine,' she said, hurriedly straightening herself out before he could check for fractures. Having his hands running over her would be the last straw.

Nothing hurt much except her head. All her bones felt intact. But her pride was in shreds. To make an exhibition of herself and then be forced to accept his help to stagger to her feet was too much.

'There is blood,' someone said, in English.

She put her hand up to her head and found her hair there wet and sticky. Her fingers came away red.

'Oh, hell . . . it's bleeding,' she muttered.

Someone in the crowd of spectators now blocking the staircase thrust a clean handkerchief at her.

Alistair, who could see who it was, said 'Thank you' and then, to Clary, 'Hold that against your head. Let's get you back to the car.' Taking hold of her arm, he gestured for people to make way.

As this whole thing was his fault, Clary longed to jerk her arm free and tell him again to go to hell. But she knew that everyone watching would get the message that she was being rude and think less of the English in consequence. Besides, as they drew aside, and she saw the long steep way down, her head started to swim and she knew that she couldn't make it unaided.

She must have looked for a moment as if she were going to faint. Before she knew what was happening, Alistair had picked her up.

'Don't make a fuss. Put your arm round my neck and hang on,' he instructed.

And because she was still feeling woozy and her head was beginning to throb where she had struck it, she did as she was told. Her eyes closed, one arm resting on his broad shoulders and the other hand pressing the folded handkerchief against her lacerated scalp, she submitted to being carried down to road level.

Considering that, although slim, she was no petite featherweight, it didn't seem to exert him.

When, at the bottom, she opened her eyes and said groggily, 'You can put me down now,' he didn't look red-faced and sweaty.

He said firmly, 'Stay where you are. I'm taking you back in the car. No arguments, please. You're in no fit state for a bus ride.'

Knowing that she wasn't, because now the throbbing in her head was becoming seriously unpleasant, Clary let him take charge.

When she woke up the following morning, Suthipong was sitting beside her. The mosquito net had been reefed into its neat daytime bundle. The sun was shining. Somewhere a bird was singing.

'Good morning. How are you feeling?' the Thai girl asked, bending towards her.

'I feel fine. What are you doing here?'

At first Clary was puzzled by Suthipong's presence in her room.

'I am waiting for you to wake up. On Mr Lincoln's instructions, we have watched you all night. He was very worried about you, even though the doctor assured him your injury was . . . superficial.' Suthipong looked pleased with herself for remembering the word and how to pronounce it.

Clary's memory came back, recalling the row at the temple, her fall, being brought back here, the doctor being sent for, murmured discussions in the background while she lay with a pounding headache, longing to be left alone and, finally, sleep. The long deep sleep of emotional and physical exhaustion.

'What time is it?' she asked.

It was past her normal getting-up time but still early.

'Mr Lincoln will be here at nine to see how you are. If you feel you can eat, I will go down and get your breakfast. Mr Lincoln has left a letter for you. It is here.'

Pointing to the bedside table, Suthipong rose from the end of the bed and disappeared on to the balcony, her bare feet moving softly over the gleaming boards.

Cautiously, Clary sat up, and was instantly made aware that yesterday's fall had left her with numerous bruises. Otherwise she felt OK. The bump on her head was still tender and would be sore for some time. But she seemed to have survived her mishap with no lasting harm done.

She put her hand out for the envelope lying on the night table on top of her bedtime reading, a well-thumbed paperback bought from the used bookshop not far from the east gate. The envelope's flap had been sealed. She slit it with a pencil and drew out a single sheet of paper. He had written on it in a clear, well-formed hand.

Dear Clary,

You have jumped to a false conclusion. What I was going to propose is that, if Nina is allowed to remain in Thailand after her release—they may insist that she leaves the country forthwith—you and she should spend two or three weeks on one of the islands in the south.

It's no use getting her out of prison and leaving her to her own devices. She needs time to recover from the experience and, even more importantly, she needs the advice and example of someone she likes to steer her away from further trouble. I certainly can't influence her and, if you are unwilling to help, she is better left where she is until I can contact her mother and let Aileen deal with the situation.

We'll discuss this further when you're feeling better. In the meantime let me assure you that although, if you were willing, I should greatly enjoy spending some time *à deux* with you, that was not what I was proposing; nor have I ever found it necessary to use threats in my relations with women.

The letter was signed *Yours, Alistair*.

She read it twice, cringing with mortification as she realised what a consummate idiot she had made of herself. How could she face him after this? How could she ever have imagined that a man as personable as Alistair would need to coerce a girl as ordinary as herself into having a fling with him?

In London there were probably girls—beautiful, glamorous girls—falling over themselves to be his playmates. She must have been out of her mind to think that he wanted her so badly that he would go to any lengths to have her.

Oh, God, what a fool he must think her! What a conceited dope! How could she look him in the eye and not feel profoundly chagrined by her own big-headed assumption that he was attracted to her as violently as she to him.

For that was the nub of the matter; although it was not until now, this minute, that she had admitted to herself that she wanted Alistair Lincoln in a way she had never before wanted any man, certainly not Miles.

But then she had been young and inexperienced when Miles had come into her life. Far too busy building a career—trying to make her father proud of her—to have had any time for love affairs.

Miles had been her first, her only lover, and for a long time she had assumed that, because he'd had other girlfriends before her, he must be practised and skilled. The suspicion that he wasn't had come later, but she had never been sure that it wasn't partly her fault that making love with him had been pleasant but never ecstatic.

After their break-up—instigated by him, not by her—it had taken her self-esteem a long time to recover. Even when she got to the stage of being able to look back at their time together with detachment, and seeing where she had gone wrong and why, she had avoided forming any new relationships.

There had been a couple of young men, backpackers like herself, who would have changed their itineraries to travel with her. But although she had liked them both, and would have been glad of their company as friends, she hadn't wanted to get involved in the way they had in mind. Both had been physically attractive, but not enough to overcome the inhibitions left over from her relationship with Miles.

It was not until the night before last, meeting Alistair, that she had felt a magnetism so disconcertingly strong that the only way to cope with it had been to deny to herself that it was happening.

But she couldn't deny it any longer. And Alistair, if he were honest, couldn't deny that yesterday afternoon, a few moments before being interrupted by the bells, he had looked at her in a way which supported the conclusion she had jumped to. She had been mistaken—but not about that burning look.

Reading the letter a third time, she wondered if it could possibly be an adroit recovery from an error of judgement.

The trouble was, she thought forlornly, that once you had trusted someone and had that trust betrayed, it was difficult to recapture your faith in human nature. You tended to regard everyone and everything with suspicion, searching for ulterior motives and devious manoeuvres.

Suthipong came back, bearing a tray on which was a pot of tea, an attractively arranged fruit salad, two fried eggs and some rice flour bread, toasted, with butter and pineapple jam.

'You will feel stronger when you have eaten. You have had nothing since lunchtime yesterday. That is too long without food,' she said, her wise and motherly tone at odds with her dewy complexion and neat school uniform.

During her travels in the East, Clary had formed the impression that young people and children in Asia were more respectful to their elders and kinder and more protective to their juniors than was general in the West.

She had seen an amusing example of the very early age at which children here became responsible while browsing in the night market the night before Alistair's arrival.

Two small and rather dirty hill tribe boys had been pottering about ahead of her when the toddler, still unsteady on his feet, had fallen over. He had been picked up and dusted down by his elder brother, a diminutive urchin who couldn't have been more than three years old himself.

Clary was smiling at the memory of his paternal manner when Suthipong, seeing the smile, said, 'The letter has made you happy. Mr Lincoln is very nice. Perhaps today he will take you for another drive in the country.'

'Today I must go to see Nina,' said Clary.

She had not yet explained to the Thai girl the connection between Alistair and Nina.

At that moment they both heard the sound of the motor scooter of Suthipong's friend Kingkarn who would give her a lift to school. Leaving Clary to enjoy her breakfast, Suthipong hurried away.

Clary was sitting on the downstairs veranda when the Mercedes glided between the gateposts and Alistair swung his long legs out of the front passenger door.

'How are you feeling this morning?'

'Much better, thank you. I'm sorry to have been such a nuisance.'

'Not at all. I blame myself for being the cause of your accident.'

His expression was concerned, but was there also a hint of amusement lurking in his eyes? She felt a wave of bright colour suffusing her face and neck.

'It wasn't your fault. It was mine... for misunderstanding. Thank you for your letter,' she said awkwardly. 'I—I should be happy to spend some time with Nina if you really think I can help her.'

'I'm sure you can. Good. That's settled...providing they don't insist on immediate deportation. How's your head? Still aching, I imagine?'

'It was a bit when I woke up, but a couple of paracetamols have cured that. But I haven't been able to shampoo my hair this morning for fear of re-starting the bleeding.' She forced herself to sound composed, although it would be a long time—if ever—before she felt comfortable with him after what had happened yesterday.

When Nina Lincoln was brought to the prison governor's office, clearly she hadn't been told that her stepbrother, Clary, and various officials would also be there.

As the younger girl came through the door, escorted by a uniformed prison officer who looked like a female wrestler, Clary felt a deep surge of relief that Alistair had arranged her release.

Nina wasn't the type to survive a long period of captivity and, by her standards, hardship. It appeared to be days since she had washed her lank blonde hair which had probably been a fashionable mane of curls when she was arrested but now looked as unkempt as dreadlocks.

Normally, in this climate, Clary washed her hair every day and felt sure that there must be facilities for Nina to do so if she wished. It was rare to see a person in Thailand who wasn't both clean and neat. It seemed unlikely that prisoners would be unable to keep clean if they wanted to. No doubt the washing facilities would be extremely primitive, but they would exist.

Possibly because the prison issue garments were too small for her, Nina had been allowed to wear her own things, and they too looked grubby and scruffy. They also showed that, unable to force down the food which she claimed was disgusting, she had lost weight, although her figure was still voluptuously curved by comparison with the slender shape of Thai girls of her age.

In her place, Clary would have felt it was politic to *wai* to the governor and the other Thais present. But obviously the respectful gesture didn't occur to Nina. At the sight of the two Europeans, her face lit up hopefully. She flashed a smile at Clary, giving a glimpse of how pretty she must have been before this happened to her. But the smile she gave Alistair was guarded and uncertain.

There was no kindness or warmth in his face as he stared at her. Rather he looked extremely stern and severe. But this, Clary knew, was the attitude he thought advisable in the circumstances.

Privately, she doubted if his expression would have been much warmer had his reunion with his stepsister taken place privately. Clearly he felt no affection for the girl and actively detested her mother.

'Well, Nina, this is a disgraceful situation you've got yourself into,' he said coldly. He paused to look her up and down as if what he saw seriously displeased him. 'However, in view of your age and the fact that you may have been led into bad ways by someone older, the authorities here have agreed to release you into my charge. Do I have your solemn promise that you will obey me in all things from now on?'

He spoke slowly, allowing the interpreter to translate what he was saying.

'I promise.' Nina's full lips quivered and her large green-gold eyes filled with tears which she managed to blink back.

Ten minutes later, sitting in the back of the Mercedes with Clary beside her and Alistair in front, she started weeping.

Clary put an arm around her. She didn't say, 'Don't cry,' because she thought tears were natural and necessary after Nina's long ordeal. She gave her a bunch of clean tissues from her bag, and sat patiently holding and patting her while she sobbed with relief at being free again.

*   *   *

'For what the hotel laundry will charge to wash and press Nina's clothes, it would be as cheap to buy her a few new things,' said Clary, unpacking the younger girl's belongings for her in the bedroom Alistair had booked for his stepsister. It was on one of the ordinary floors, not in the Executive Club, but it was still quite luxurious.

At the sight of it Nina had collapsed in another flood of tears.

'You can't imagine . . . how terrible it was in th-that p-place,' she had gasped, between sobs. 'I was going crazy in there! If you hadn't got me out, I'd have k-killed myself, Alistair.'

'Nonsense,' he had said briskly. 'Pull yourself together, Nina.'

Now she was in the bathroom, up to her neck in a warm bubble bath, and he was standing by the window which, to Clary's relief, was on the opposite side of the building from his suite and did not have a view of Doi Suthep and the Wat Phra That temple not far from its summit.

'I agree. It would be much better to throw out all that tat and replace it with new kit. But I'd rather you shopped for her, if you feel up to it?'

'Certainly, and I think you're right. Nina needs a day or two of quiet adjustment to her release before she starts mixing with people and leading a normal life.'

'Possibly, but that wasn't why I suggested it. She may be out of prison, but she's still in the doghouse and I don't want her to forget it. Also you have much better taste in clothes than she has.' He looked with disfavour at the typically trendy teenage garments laid out on the bed. 'Buy her the sort of things you wear.

While you're out shopping for her, I have a lot of questions to ask that young woman.' He took his billfold from his back pocket and took out several thousand-*baht* notes. 'Will that be enough?'

'One of those will be ample,' said Clary. 'Don't be *too* hard on her, Alistair, will you? I think she's had as much as she can take.'

The set of his mouth remained grim. 'I know Nina better than you do. She has a short memory. Don't be too sympathetic or this time next week she'll have forgotten about being in prison and be up to some new mischief.'

He glanced at his watch. 'While you're out, I'll call Thai Airways and check out the flight situation.'

Presently, leaving the hotel to walk to the nearby market where, with some good-humoured haggling, she ought to be able to kit Nina out for the equivalent of five or six pounds, Clary wondered if Alistair was right or if his stepsister's traumatic experience had been a lasting lesson to her.

One thing was certain. Now that he had achieved the object of his trip, he was unlikely to hang about. Coming down in the lift with some departing guests, she had gathered that they were catching the midnight flight from Bangkok to London.

It was possible that Alistair would also leave on that flight. Within a few hours he might have swept out of her life as abruptly as he had entered it. Which, for her peace of mind, would be much the best thing.

So why did she feel so downcast at the thought of saying goodbye to him?

CHAPTER FIVE

WHEN Clary returned to Nina's room, carrying several plastic bags, and the younger girl opened the door, she was wrapped in a large white bath towel.

'As I can't go out without clothes, I was watching the in-house movie, but it isn't much good,' she said, switching it off. 'When I finished in the bathroom, I found Alistair had thrown out all my clothes . . . given them to the maid and told her to junk them. That's typical of him. He always did ride roughshod on everyone. Not that I mind, as it happens—all my things stank of the prison. He said you were getting me some new stuff.'

Clary dumped her parcels on the bed. Her head was aching again.

'Far from riding roughshod over the Thai officials, as well as paying that huge fine, Alistair had to be extremely diplomatic to persuade them to release you so quickly,' she said quietly. 'You'll never be able to repay what he's done for you, Nina. Where is he?'

'Gone up to his suite to fix this trip to some island. Sounds nice. I'm sure you and I will get along fine, Clary. The person I'm most grateful to is you, you know. If it hadn't been for you . . .' Nina shuddered. 'I can't bear to think about that. What have you brought me?'

'A couple of T-shirts, some jeans, a pair of shorts, a swimsuit . . .' Clary unpacked the bags. 'If anything's the wrong size, the stallholders have promised to change it.'

Nina loosened the towel and let it fall to the floor, revealing that in spite of the weight she had lost her breasts were still a lot fuller than Clary's, her hips more generously curved.

'I never wear a bra,' she said, seeing that her new wardrobe included three pairs of cotton micro-briefs and a couple of light bras.

'Oh, don't you? I would if I had your nice figure and wanted to keep it that way,' said Clary. 'They say that not wearing a bra is a fast way to end up saggy.'

'Really? I didn't know that. Are you sure?'

'That's the experts' opinion.'

'Maybe I should wear one, then. I'd hate to sag,' said Nina, pulling a face.

So it was a transformed Nina who accompanied Clary upstairs when Alistair summoned them to lunch in his suite. Clary had bought her some bright plastic spring-clips to control her wild mop of hair. Under a plain white T-shirt, her breasts were restrained by a bra. And her new pale blue jeans had no deliberate slashes in them like the pair he had thrown out.

'Better . . . much better,' was his verdict, when he had inspected her. He turned to Clary. 'All internal flights are heavily booked until the end of this month. We have no option but to leave here first thing tomorrow, and the only available flight to Phuket is at eight-thirty in the evening, which means nine hours to kill in Bangkok, but it can't be helped.'

'But why do we need to go to Phuket?' she asked. 'Surely that's the big touristy island off the west coast? I thought we'd be going to my island . . . Koh Samui off the east coast.'

'I've done some checking and Koh Phi Phi in the Andaman Sea sounds a more suitable place for Nina to recuperate. It's smaller than Koh Samui, with excellent swimming and snorkelling and other islands close by for a change of scene. It's all laid on...a hotel close to Phuket airport for tomorrow night and the next day a short bus journey to the docks near Phuket Town followed by a two-hour sea crossing to the island. All being well, the day after tomorrow lunch will be freshly caught fish in a palm-thatched beach bar.'

'That sounds great,' said Nina enthusiastically. 'Give me the beach scene any time. You can keep the hill scene as far as I'm concerned,' she added, looking out of the window at the haze-veiled mass of Doi Suthep. 'I never did like this place, and now...the sooner I get out of here the better.'

Clary said nothing. The arrangements Alistair had made meant they had the rest of today in his company and most of tomorrow. Presumably he would spend the time in Bangkok with them, then see them off on their flight to Phuket before catching the midnight flight to Europe. By the time they were settled in Koh Phi Phi, he would be back in London, doing whatever he did there. She still didn't know what it was and this wasn't the moment to ask. Perhaps what she knew about him now would be all she would ever know.

After lunch he suggested spending the afternoon by the hotel pool. While buying a swimsuit for Nina, Clary had chosen one for herself. So she didn't have to go back to the guesthouse to fetch her old one-piece which was beginning to lose its elasticity.

Alistair was already stretched out on a sun-bed when the two girls joined him on the pool terrace off the

second floor. Naked except for a brief dark red
bathing slip, his body looked even more powerful
without being in any way beefy. He was muscled as
sleekly as a cat . . . one of the big cats, she thought.
When his tall frame was relaxed one noticed the good
proportions, the quick-tanning olive skin which went
with his dark hair. It was only when he moved that
the ripple of sinews caught the eye.

There were two vacant beds on his left. Nina tossed
her pool towel on the one farthest from him, leaving
Clary the one in the middle. Aware that her figure
did not show to advantage beside Nina's, she spread
her towel over the lounger next to Alistair's, knowing
that he was watching her and feeling absurdly self-
conscious considering that her new suit was far less
revealing than those of the other women there.

Nina's tan had faded during her weeks in prison
and Clary had bought some sun lotion for her in the
market.

'Shall I do your back for you?' she asked.

'Yes, please.' Nina lay face down and reached
behind her to unclip the top of her two-piece.

As Clary finished applying the lotion to the younger
girl's back, Alistair said, 'Would you like me to do
your back?'

'Er . . . no, thanks.' When he raised a questioning
eyebrow, she added, 'I'm going in for a swim first,
and anyway I'm brown enough not to burn easily.'

'Yes, you have a very nice tan.' His eyes, slightly
narrowed against the strong light, swept over her, re-
newing her self-consciousness.

All the loungers were close to the pool's edge, so
it would have been inconsiderate to dive in and
perhaps sprinkle drops of water on the warm skins of

the sunbathers. Clary entered the pool by the ladder and swam back and forth several times, using the breast stroke and keeping her injury out of the water. She still felt a bit shaken up, partly physically, and partly emotionally. She knew that she wouldn't be at peace as long as Alistair was with them. He was a most disturbing, unsettling influence.

As she turned to do another length, she saw him descending the ladder. With three long-armed strokes he was standing in front of her so that she had to stop swimming and put her feet to the floor.

'As we have an early start tomorrow, it might be a good idea for you to check out of your place later today and spend the night here,' he suggested. 'The hotel is full, I believe, but Nina's room has twin beds. Would you mind sharing with her just for one night?'

'Not at all, if she doesn't mind.'

'Why should she? She's damn lucky to be here. I hope you aren't disappointed at not going to Koh Samui as you planned, but I made some enquiries about it and it sounds the kind of place where you could have problems with her. Samui has a paved road and motorbikes for hire, I'm told. I don't want Nina roaring off on some tearaway's pillion.'

'I can't see her doing that,' said Clary.

'Can't you? I can. It's a rule of life that people repeat their mistakes. My impression of Nina, now that I've talked to her, is that she's very like her mother but without Aileen's shrewdness. I'd bet money that Nina will go through life being picked up by untrustworthy men and sooner or later ditched by them.'

His put up a hand to rake back his wet hair from which crystal beads of water were sliding down his long neck to shoulders which seemed even broader at these close quarters.

'Have you repeated your mistakes?' Clary asked.

He grinned at her, showing his good teeth. 'I haven't made any...so far. Minor misjudgements, yes, of course. Nothing serious.'

'Bully for you,' she said, with a touch of sarcasm. 'Most people make a lot of mistakes in a lifetime...especially at Nina's age.'

His blue gaze was suddenly too intent for her comfort. 'Did you?'

'Yes, I made a couple.' But she wasn't going to tell him what they were.

She slept badly and from four o'clock onwards lay awake, trying not to think about the man now asleep on a higher floor.

Instead she thought about the handkerchief someone had given her on the Stairway to Heaven and which Suthipong, thinking it was Clary's, had washed out for her, removing most but not all the bloodstains on it.

Clary had a feeling that before she applied it to her cut head it had been a new and perhaps Sunday best, special occasion handkerchief. In Europe, unless it were exquisitely hand-embroidered or edged with fine hand-made lace, a hanky was not a thing of great value. But here, where some people were so desperately poor that a beggar would give a deep *wai* for a five-*baht* coin dropped into his tin by a passerby, the loss of even a mass-produced handkerchief might be a matter for regret. She wished there were some way she could thank its owner for the kind gesture and give them a replacement. But how?

At six o'clock the telephone rang and she listened to a recorded wake-up message before throwing back the blanket, sandwiched between two fine quality sheets, made necessary by the air-conditioning.

In the other bed, Nina groaned and snuggled deeper under the bedclothes.

'I'll have my shower first to give you time to surface,' said Clary.

The response was the grumpy mumble of someone who hated early rising.

This morning, being very careful round the area where the skin had broken, Clary washed her hair. The bathroom had a built-in hair dryer, but it wasn't as effective as her portable dryer, so she plugged that into a socket at the back of the dressing table in the bedroom. Nina was still an inert shape under the clothes, and the whining noise of the dryer at its fast speed made her give another protesting groan.

At first Clary tried to coax her to get up. Then, at the very moment when she was beginning to get exasperated, the telephone rang.

She picked up the receiver. 'Hello?'

'Alistair here. Is Nina up?'

'She will be in a minute.'

'She should be up now. Let me speak to her.'

Two minutes later Nina was out of bed and in the shower and Clary was blow-drying her hair and thinking about the short, sharp tirade which had proved so much more effective than her gentler urging.

Would she be able to manage Nina without Alistair's back-up? Clearly, however much his step-sister might resent his arbitrary ways, she was more than a little afraid of him. Would she try to take advantage of Clary when the two of them were on their own?

The airport restaurant at Chiang Mai had a sophisticated aubergine colour scheme with groups and pairs of white elephants inside lighted glass cases as the main decorative motif. Smartly uniformed waiters and waitresses in what her mother would have called shocking pink, and Clary now thought of as Thai pink, provided table service.

She understood the significance of the white elephant motif and wondered if Nina did. But, as she was about to explain that in Thailand white elephants symbolised peace and prosperity and were always presented to the King, having been a prerogative of the monarch for many centuries, she changed her mind. Nina might not be interested in the customs of the country. She didn't want to bore her.

From the window table where they were having coffee, they saw their aircraft land on the runway and then taxi to a position which gave them a dress circle view of the service vehicles converging on it. First the stairs for the passengers to walk down were positioned against the front and rear doors, then a train of four empty trolleys snaked towards the baggage hold, then containers of food and mail arrived to replace the ones taken off.

Even before she saw her navy blue backpack among the luggage to be loaded, Clary had a curious sense of time running out. It would have been understandable if later today *she* had been returning to Europe. But she wasn't. She was only midway through her travels and wouldn't have to face the cold and grey skies of her homeland until about this time next year, preferably after the European spring had begun.

It wasn't until they boarded that she found she was about to have her first experience of flying first class.

'Where are we going?' asked Nina as, not much more than an hour later, they sat, three abreast, in the back of an airport limousine on the highway leading to Bangkok.

Clary already knew their specific destination. She had heard Alistair say to the driver, 'Oriental Hotel, please' and had blushed at the memory of storming at him, 'I wouldn't spend two weeks with you if you offered me a suite at the Oriental, sapphires for breakfast and rubies for tea, Mr Lincoln!'

Now, sitting beside him in the back of the spacious, air-conditioned car, she flushed again as he answered his stepsister's question.

'To the Oriental, one of the world's great hotels, although it's changed a lot since Somerset Maugham and Joseph Conrad used to stay there. I suppose those two famous writers are not even names to you, Nina, but presumably you've heard of Barbara Cartland and Wilbur Smith...perhaps even of Gore Vidal. They've all stayed at the Oriental and had suites named in their honour. As Clary is more bookish than you are, I thought she would like to spend the day in a hotel with so many literary associations.'

'Has it got a swimming pool?' asked Nina.

'Two pools, I believe...and no doubt a shop selling sapphires and rubies,' he added.

Nina looked puzzled by this remark. Clary's cheeks burned at his teasing. She knew if she looked at him she would see a bright gleam of mockery in his eyes.

He was sitting in the nearside corner and she turned to look out of the offside window, hoping he would see only the edge of the blush which was making her face flame.

'I've stayed at other hotels in the same group,' Alistair went on, 'the Excelsior in Hong Kong and the Singapore Oriental, but I haven't been here before. Like everywhere else in Thailand, they're extremely booked up at the moment, but I managed to get a room in the River Wing so that we can use the pool and have somewhere private to relax. Is there anything you would particularly like to do while you're in Bangkok, Clary? I'll keep Nina company if you'd like to go shopping.'

'There is one thing I'd like to do. It shouldn't take more than an hour,' she said, her raised colour subsiding.

'Then by all means go ahead and do it. Perhaps later in the day we might take a trip up the Chao Phraya. I'm told that walking round the city is made pretty unpleasant by the noise and fumes of the traffic, but that shouldn't apply to the river.'

Although, sealed inside the limousine, they were shielded from the pollution and the roar of Bangkok's teeming traffic, as they entered the city it did seem that Thailand's capital, once known as the Venice of the East because of its network of canals, had lost most of its charm when the *klongs* were replaced by roads.

At least that was Clary's impression before they arrived at the Oriental Hotel.

But when the car glided up the slope to the hotel's portico, a white-uniformed doorman sprang to open the rear door, and Alistair got out and offered his hand to help her out, she knew at once she was about to step into a world where the charm of Bangkok had survived.

For one thing, the bell-boys here wore the traditional *phaakamaa*, here a length of dark blue silk worn in the style of a sarong but with the difference that it was drawn between the legs to give the appearance of knickerbockers. The combination of dark blue with white tunics, white stockings and well-polished black shoes looked very smart indeed.

Unlike many hotels where the first thing to be seen was the reception desk, here the doors led into a lounge the size of a small cathedral and with a view of the gardens and swimming pools and, beyond them, the broad Chao Phraya, the famous River of Kings.

The reception, enquiry and cashier's desks, and the lifts, flanked by two large black statues of elephants, were located round to the right where there was much coming and going of important-looking people leaving their room keys, picking up mail, asking if flights had been confirmed and having their problems smoothed out by dapper assistant managers with flowers in their buttonholes and pretty multi-lingual girls.

Feeling very much a fish out of water—for although, in the years with Miles, she had been to expensive hotels it was a long time ago and none of them had been quite as glamorous as the Oriental— Clary stood by while Alistair registered.

Then the three of them were escorted up to the fourth floor by a suave, dark-suited man who was merely polite to the girls but extremely deferential to Alistair. Who *was* Alistair? Clary wondered, not for the first time. Clearly someone whose name meant more to the hotel management than it did to her.

The first thing which caught her eye when they entered Room 403 was the unusual curtain material with its pattern of rippling water and lotus flowers. When the long, full curtains were swept aside by their escort, a superb view of the river was revealed.

'I'm sorry we're unable to provide you and the young ladies with separate accommodation, Mr Lincoln, but you'll find three of our pool robes and extra towels in the bathroom. I hope you and your sister and her friend enjoy your short stay with us. Please let us know if there's any way we can make your visit more comfortable.'

Their escort bowed himself out, leaving the door open because their luggage was arriving.

'You told them I was your sister? I am honoured,' Nina said pertly, after the porter had been tipped and gone away.

She had flung herself down on one of the wide twin beds pushed close together and sharing an imposing headboard. Their covers matched the curtains and they each had one of the triangular backrests, made from tightly stuffed cylinders of fabric, against which Thai people had leaned before the introduction of Western furniture.

'If you want to sprawl on the bed, take your shoes and the cover off first,' Alistair ordered crisply. 'I told them you were my sister, when I telephoned about a room, merely to regularise the situation, not because I've changed my view of our non-existent relationship.' He opened a wood-panelled door which proved to be the room's refrigerated honour bar. 'Would you like a cold drink, Clary?'

She shook her head. 'If you'll excuse me, I'll go and attend to my errand. It shouldn't take long.'

'Don't lose your way. If you're not back by one o'clock, we'll send out a search party.' The contrast between his smile and his manner towards her and his critical attitude to Nina was very marked.

'I'll come with you,' announced the younger girl.

'No, you won't. You'll stay here,' he told her abruptly. 'Off you go, Clary.' He moved to the door and opened it for her. 'I expect we'll be by the pool when you get back.'

Waiting for the lift in the thickly carpeted corridor, Clary had a feeling that now she was out of the way Nina would be subjected to a severe dressing-down. Perhaps it was not undeserved, for she did have some irritating ways and very little respect for her luxurious surroundings, considering how recently she had been rescued from squalid ones.

At the same time Alistair was being a bit hard on her. Clearly, in many respects he was a hard man with no time for weaker mortals.

One of the lifts opened and Clary stepped inside. Probably if he knew the nature of her business in the city, he would consider it an unnecessary waste of time and effort, she thought. But it was something she felt she must do.

The next time she used the lift to get down to the lobby, she was wearing a blue cotton robe with the hotel's logo, an open fan, embroidered on the pocket. Under it was her swimsuit and on her feet were navy blue quilted cotton mules also supplied by the hotel.

In the lobby she crossed to the glass doors which slid open at her approach and gave on to a wide arcade with the windows of a jeweller's shop on one side and a well-kept garden on the other.

Clary paused to look at the display of rings, bracelets and necklaces set with precious stones, mainly diamonds, rubies and sapphires. But although they were obviously ornaments of the highest quality and extremely expensive, they didn't appeal to her as much as the cheap silver rings, set with moonstones and low-grade amethysts, she had bought herself while in Bali.

She had seen from the window of the bedroom, which looked down on the pool, that Alistair and Nina were lying on green chaises-longues spread with orange towels on the side of the pool nearest the Authors' Wing.

But in the time it had taken her to come down to ground level Alistair had left his chaise and was now in the water which, unlike the small pool yesterday, here was long enough to allow him to swim a fast crawl.

As she paused at the end of the pool to watch his back muscles flexing and glistening in the sun, she was approached by an attendant carrying towels.

'Where would you like to sit, *madame*?'

Clary indicated the group of loungers where Nina was lying and followed the man round the edge of the pool. Alistair was swimming the other way now, his strong arms rising and falling in a steady rhythm, his head only turning to snatch in a fresh breath of air on every fourth stroke.

The style and speed with which he was cleaving the water sent a strange tremor through the pit of her stomach. She found herself wondering if he made love as superbly as he swam. Not that a splendid body and all that controlled power was any guarantee that he would be wonderful in bed. It could be that Alistair was as mechanical and unimaginative as Miles. Anyway, she would never find out, didn't wish to find out.

In a few hours he would be gone, and she was glad of it ... wasn't she?

CHAPTER SIX

THEY had lunch at Ciao, one of the hotel's two river-side terrace restaurants, with a table at the water's edge.

Behind the marble terrace with its central fountain and lily pool, the elegant façade of the Authors' Wing could be seen through the trunks of the palms which shaded the garden between it and where they were sitting. This was the original hotel where Maugham and Conrad had stayed long ago, now dwarfed by modern additions.

Ciao, as its name suggested, specialised in pizzas and ice creams. Clary chose the wholemeal pizza and then, while the others were still looking at the menu, turned her attention to the river and the many different types of boats coming and going on this wide section of the Chao Phraya which she knew wasn't far from its mouth.

'The river here must be tidal,' said Alistair, after ordering their lunch. 'Those mats of vegetation are travelling upstream, and at quite a rate of knots. I wonder what that stuff is?'

'Could they be lotus plants?' Clary suggested.

Alistair made a sign to the head waiter who, when asked, told them the plants were water hyacinths, which were something of a problem as they spread very fast and could soon block the smaller waterways leading off the river.

Nina wasn't interested in any of this. She was looking about at the other lunchers. 'Gee, everyone here is so *old*,' she said fretfully.

Clary said, 'Most young people can't afford all this glamour. We're lucky to be here. It's a glimpse of a world we would never normally see...thanks to Alistair.'

'There are some younger people staying here. I saw what looked like the members of a pop group checking in earlier,' he said. 'And probably there are quite a number of honeymooners.'

At that moment a party of people in their early twenties arrived. Clary judged them to be well-heeled Americans, three men and a girl who looked like the sister of one of them. As they paused to look round and choose one of the vacant tables, Nina perked up. When one of the men noticed her, her interest in him was as clear to Clary as it must have been to the young man. But Alistair was watching a pair of rice barges being towed by a tugboat and didn't see the exchange of looks.

Towards the end of lunch he repeated his earlier suggestion that they should take a trip on the river. Clary was enthusiastic, but Nina said she would rather spend the afternoon relaxing by the pool.

Somewhat to Clary's surprise, Alistair didn't insist on her coming with them.

'You may want something to read from the shop in the lobby.' He gave her some money. 'Cold drinks you can sign for, but stick to fruit punch. We don't want to come back and find you cross-eyed from that mixture of rum and *crème de menthe* they call an Oriental Cooler!'

*   *   *

The sound of its engine reduced to a low purr, the tour boat glided along the canal, giving the passengers glimpses of Thai domestic life in a quiet residential area somewhere to the west of the river.

'You were right: this is much, much nicer than plodding round the city centre,' Clary murmured to Alistair, remembering how hot and noisy it had been on her short excursion into the heart of Bangkok before lunch.

The boat had room for about twenty passengers, and she and Alistair were sharing one of the front seats so that he had room to stretch his long legs. Although she was fascinated by what they were seeing, at the same time she was very much aware of his nearness and his arm lying along the backrest behind her shoulders.

The *klong* they were following was about the same width as a suburban road in London. Leading off it were narrower waterways navigable only in a small rowing boat, some of them made impassable by thickets of water hyacinths.

Although Clary felt it was an invasion of their privacy to have boatloads of tourists passing by every day, the people on the verandas of the houses along the bank didn't seem to mind. A few ignored the passing boat. One or two were asleep on their verandas. But mostly they smiled and the children waved.

Here and there were shops which the woman sitting behind Clary told her husband reminded her of corner shops in England when she was a child. On the little jetty in front of one of these small general stores, a Thai housewife wearing a sun-faded *phaasin* wrapped round her from waist to ankle, with Western-style blouse, was holding her purchase in one hand and the painter of her boat in the other while she chatted to the shopkeeper.

Unlike an English suburb, where the houses in a street were usually occupied by people of much the same social and financial standing, here there was a much greater variety, ranging from neglected wooden shacks whose occupants were obviously poor, to large modern houses with all the hallmarks of nouveau riche ownership. In between these two extremes were many attractive family houses of weathered timber with lots of greenery on their verandas and often a small private pier just large enough to accommodate two park-type benches built facing each other, with a roof to shade them.

Presently the boat returned to the Chao Phraya and tied up alongside a building with a large veranda where drinks and snacks were waiting. Sipping an unexpectedly strong whisky and water, Clary remembered Alistair's instructions to Nina to stay off the more potent mixtures served from the pool bar by a steward with as much gold braid on his sleeves as an admiral. Maybe by now Nina had found someone to keep her company or had even gone out to explore. It was odd that Alistair hadn't made her come with them. Could it be that he had wanted to have her, Clary, to himself?

No, it couldn't, she decided. A more likely explanation was that he had known a trip like this would bore Nina and he didn't want to have his own pleasure spoiled by his stepsister looking glum.

'Are you beginning to regret agreeing to chaperon Nina?' he asked suddenly, startling her with his insight into her thoughts.

'No, but I do have some doubts about my ability to handle her.'

They were standing a little apart from the rest of the passengers, most of whom were comparing notes on other sightseeing excursions they had been on.

With no one close enough to overhear, Alistair said, 'I'm sure that if Nina thought she was being propositioned, she wouldn't flare up as you did the other day. I should think she's had plenty of passes made at her, and been in a lot of men's beds. With a mother as promiscuous as Aileen, it's not surprising.'

His reference—the second today—to the episode at Wat Phra That made her colour.

'You don't *know* that Nina's had a lot of experience.'

'I don't *know* that you haven't, but intelligent guesswork tells me that whatever relationships you've had have never been casual affairs, certainly not one-night stands.'

'Not likely!' Clary said roundly. 'That's like playing Russian roulette—and even if it weren't, it wouldn't be my style,' she added. 'To me making love should be an expression of deep feeling, not a trivial pleasure like . . . like this drink.'

'I agree,' Alistair answered.

She had thought he might say something flip, and was both relieved and disconcerted by the seriousness of his reply.

To her even greater surprise, she found herself saying, 'You may agree in theory, but can you say, hand on heart, that you've never made love to someone you weren't at the very least fond of?'

He sipped his drink, looking thoughtful. She wondered if, to answer her question, he had to cast his mind back a long way, over numerous affairs with women, few of any importance in his life.

'No, I can't truthfully say that,' he answered. 'I have to admit there was a time when, like most young males, if there'd been no health risks, I should have jumped into bed with any and every willing female. That I didn't was due to a strong sense of self-preservation rather than high principles,' he went on drily. 'But after a while any man with intelligence arrives at the realisation that sex is much more enjoyable if there's ... not necessarily love, but certainly affection.'

Lifting his glass to his lips again, he drained the last of his whisky. 'I think they want us to start boarding the barge for the return trip,' he said, looking over her head.

Aboard the old-fashioned barge, now used to take passengers back to the landing stages where they had boarded the long narrow canal boat, another selection of things to eat had been set out on a table, and trays of drinks were being handed round.

'How very kind of your husband to give me a helping hand.'

A large middle-aged woman with a game leg who had come on the trip on her own sat down next to Clary, who had become separated from Alistair while they were boarding. Now he was having a look at the food on the table.

'He's not my husband ... just a friend,' she explained.

'Oh ... well, he has very nice manners. I'm all right on the flat, but I need a bit of assistance getting on and off boats,' the woman confided. She laughed. 'Shouldn't care to fall in and swallow this river water, although I was struck by the absence of unpleasant smells along the canals. I've been in towns in Europe

where the smells are much worse than here... Bruges
for one. In hot weather I've known the canals there
to stink to high heaven!'

For the rest of the journey downstream, the woman
talked almost non-stop about her travels round the
world while Alistair plied her and Clary with nutty
biscuits and small, fat, delicious bananas.

Some distance upriver from the Oriental pier, the
barge put some passengers off at the landing steps at
River City. Clary had read about this large multi-
storey shopping complex in the booklet *Welcome to
the Oriental* which was on the dressing table in Room
403. So, it appeared, had Alistair.

He said, 'Let's get off here and have a look round
the place, shall we?'

Saying goodbye to their lame acquaintance, he took
Clary by the hand and hurried her ashore.

The interior of River City consisted of a huge atrium
with escalators rising to the surrounding floors. They
started at the top where there was a concentration of
antique shops.

There were several beautiful things Clary would
have liked to buy had she had the money and a place
of her own to go back to. She particularly liked a
small standing Buddha figure. The dealer, scenting
interest, said it was a Khmer antique brought in from
Kampuchea and therefore, unlike a Thai Buddha, it
could be exported.

Had she not been with Alistair, Clary doubted if
the dealer would have bothered to put aside his paper
and point out his choicest wares. If she'd entered the
shop on her own, he would have sized her up and
judged, correctly, that she was merely looking at
things far beyond her purse.

But even in a cotton sports shirt, Alistair had the look of a man of means and, in one of the shops they looked round, he proved it by buying a pair of Chinese cloisonné dogs, the enamel a vibrant mixture of dark and light blue.

Even though he succeeded in getting the price down from astronomical to very expensive, it still made Clary's mind boggle, not only at the kind of income which could run to such costly trifles but at his confidence in his own taste and judgement.

Also she couldn't help remembering the child she had seen in the street that morning; a boy of about ten years old with a bright, intelligent face but both legs horribly deformed. He had been sitting on the pavement begging and had *wai*-ed his thanks for the coin she had dropped in his tin. Many of the people passing, Thais and tourists, had ignored him.

Clary had gone on her way, horrified by his plight and ashamed that her pity for him wasn't strong enough to make her do something about it. For surely there must be *something* which could be done? Some place where he could be educated for a better life than begging?

If I had Alistair's money, I *would* do something, she thought. But she knew that was an excuse to ease her troubled conscience. If she had truly cared about the boy she would have found some way of helping him.

Alistair bought other things; a pair of pale grey-green celadon lamp bases which he intended to give as a wedding present to a friend who was getting married, some ornate silver boxes to put by for Christmas and birthday presents, and a number of antique baskets. Instead of having them packed to take on the plane, he asked for them to be shipped back to London.

On the floor below more antique shops were interspersed with shops selling silk and leather goods. But when he asked if she wanted to look at dresses or shoes, Clary shook her head.

'I'd love a cup of tea—I'm not used to drinking whisky in the middle of the afternoon. But perhaps we ought to get back. If Nina saw the barge returning, she may be wondering what's happened to us.'

'I doubt it. Nina would only do that if she were bored. If she's had enough of lying by the pool, working on her tan, she's probably trying on clothes in the hotel's shops, or possibly having a hairdo and manicure which she'll have put on the bill, or she may be catching up on the sundaes she missed in prison. She always had a sweet tooth and, when she was younger, a bad skin . . . not a flawless complexion like yours.'

'Thank you.' The compliment kindled a glow of pleasure inside her.

There was a comfortable café on the first floor. While they were drinking tea, Clary said, 'Now that you've questioned Nina, do you still disbelieve her story about what happened?'

'I was sceptical at first, but I think she's probably telling the truth. But the chances of ever tracking down this guy Sean, and proving that he let her carry the can for him, are so slim as to be non-existent. She swears that she didn't know he'd bought some *ganja*. It seems very possible he did it when she wasn't watching—had gone to the loo, perhaps—knew there was a risk of being shopped to the police by the vendor, and slipped the stuff in her tote bag as a precaution in case they were stopped on the way back to the guesthouse. Which was precisely what happened. I'm not a violent man, but I must say I'd give a lot to get my hands on that bastard.'

'I know how you feel. We can only hope that one day he'll get his come-uppance. He must be as low as they come.' Even lower than Miles, and what he did to me was rotten enough, Clary thought, remembering it.

'Nevertheless, it was partly her own fault for trusting him,' Alistair went on. 'She hadn't known him long when it happened and still doesn't know much about him.'

'I don't know much about you, but I'd trust you not to slip something incriminating in my bag while I was in the Ladies',' said Clary.

'But I didn't pick you up in a bar, and you wouldn't let me sleep with you...' he paused before adding '...which I gather was the state of play at the time of Nina's arrest.'

Had he paused deliberately, to tease her? she wondered. Did he guess that when he spoke of sleeping with her, it made her pulses race, her heart beat a fast tattoo?

Trying to sound composed, she said, 'I'm eight years older than Nina. It makes a difference. Perhaps she had fallen for him. Girls do lose their heads over men. It happens all the time.'

'And not only girls,' was Alistair's sardonic comment. 'My father lost his head over Aileen. He was fifty-three when he met her and somehow he made himself believe that she cared about him...an overweight middle-aged man with bifocals and a bald

patch. He was also the chairman of a large engineering company, but he persuaded himself that had
nothing to do with it. Aileen was twenty-five, with
expensive tastes.' He gave an expressive shrug.

Clary refilled his cup, her heart full of compassion
for the teenage Alistair who had had to watch his
father making a fool of himself.

'The reason, of course,' he went on, 'wasn't only
that Aileen set out to seduce him and had all the qual-
ities needed to send a middle-aged widower off his
rocker, but he had never been young. His father
worked on a factory floor, died young and left Dad
with his widowed mother and four younger children
to fend for. When he married, he put off having
children until his brothers and sisters were launched
in the world and until he'd started to make money.
Then he and my mother found they couldn't have
children, so they adopted me.'

Clary began to see that the reasons for Alistair's
lack of affection for Nina were more complicated than
she had realised. As an adopted son he would, presumably, have been even more wary of contenders for
his father's love than a natural son.

'You have a sympathetic face, Clary,' he told her.
'The past, as somebody said, is "another country"...
I don't often talk about it.'

'Do you know who your natural parents were?' she
ventured to ask.

He shook his head. 'No. Nor do I wish to. I should
think I was illegitimate. Thirty-six years ago there
weren't as many support systems for single parents as
there are now. I guess my father didn't want to know
and my mother couldn't cope, so she left me outside

an orphanage. Sounds like a Victorian melodrama, but it still happens occasionally.'

She found it hard to believe that this self-assured, dynamic man had had such an unpromising start in life. 'Was it a well-run orphanage?' she asked.

'Very. I have no unhappy memories of early childhood. When I was seven I was adopted by Geoffrey and Mary Lincoln and from then on had every advantage that money can buy, plus the support and affection of two of the best people one could wish to know. But unfortunately Mary died in her middle forties and a few years later Geoffrey met Aileen and was foolish enough to marry her and have Nina's surname changed to his.'

'Are you certain her mother was unfaithful to him?' Clary asked.

His blue eyes were suddenly bleak, all kindness and humour fled from a face which had hardened into a mask of contempt. 'Positive,' he said curtly. 'When I was twenty, she had a go at me . . . came to my room in a transparent robe . . . poured out a sob story about marrying Dad for Nina's sake . . . and how the pills he was taking for his high blood pressure had finished him sexually. It was cleverly done. She guessed he hadn't long to go, knew I was his principal heir and wanted me in her clutches as firmly as he was.'

Clary remembered what he had told her during the refreshment stop on the river trip: that as a very young man he had lusted after many women but had been restrained by the hazards involved. At twenty, still living under his father's roof, he wouldn't have found it easy to resist a beautiful woman—even his father's wife—who was hell-bent on having him.

'So now you know why I wasn't keen to come out here and get involved with Nina and Aileen. As far as I'm concerned they're bad news and always have been.'

'Yes, I understand,' said Clary.

But what she still didn't know, and couldn't ask him, was if he had thrown Aileen out on the night she had tried to seduce him. Or had he succumbed to her wiles so that now his contempt for her was aggravated by shame and self-loathing?

Looking at him now, an experienced man in his middle thirties, she couldn't imagine any woman, however alluring, being able to influence him. But at twenty, only one year older than Nina was now, he would have been far more vulnerable.

'So now you know most of my life story, but I still know almost nothing about you,' he said, his face resuming its normal expression.

'My history is terribly dull. A suburban childhood. Parents who play bridge and garden . . . and were appalled when I announced that I was going to backpack my way round Asia.'

'What were you doing before you made that decision?'

'Working in an office in London. Then I lost my job in one of those corporate upheavals which make headlines every so often. It felt like a disaster at the time, but since then I've realised that being forced to re-think my future was a good thing. I've seen and learnt more since I started my travels than in the whole rest of my life.'

'There was no man in your life?'

'There had been, but it was over. With my job gone, I had no personal commitments to keep me in England.'

Once she wouldn't have been able to say that without bitterness creeping into her voice. But now she could mention it lightly, even with a certain amusement at the literal truth of her statement.

When she had stopped being a yuppie, upwardly mobile, when it was clear that losing her job wasn't merely a hiccup in her career but a prolonged hiatus, Miles had politely but firmly thrown her out. Out of their flat which, legally, had been his flat, and out of his carefully planned life.

'And no present plans to go back?' Alistair asked.

'Not for at least a year. That's when my funds will run out. What I'll do then I don't know. I'm not even thinking about it. I'm living each day as it comes...letting the future take care of itself.'

He gave her a long intent look and she wondered what he was thinking but was somehow afraid to ask.

'That's always a good idea,' was his comment on her last remark. '"Look thy last on all things lovely, Every hour..." I learned that at school, but can't remember who wrote it.' He glanced at his watch. 'We'd better be moving.'

Now it was rush-hour on the river. All the water-buses were crowded with uniformed students and office workers going home. But they managed to jump on board a crowded boat as it stopped by the River City steps and stood in the crush at the stern for the short trip down-river to the Oriental pier.

When their boat bounced on the wash of another craft going fast in the opposite direction, Clary felt Alistair's hand on her waist, steadying her. Being with him gave her a curious feeling of safety. Not that she felt in danger when she was on her own, but she didn't feel the extra security that his tall presence gave her. If she missed her footing jumping ashore, he would be there to grab her. If the boat sank—unlikely contingency!—he would be in the water beside her.

But in a few hours we shall have said goodbye, was her next thought. I shall write to him from Phi Phi Island about Nina, and receive a message from him when he finds out where her mother is. But that will be all. That will be the end of it. Perhaps that's why he unburdened himself in the café...because we shall never meet again.

And, deep down, she knew it was better so. Because Alistair Lincoln was a danger to her. A few more days in his company and who knew what folly she might not commit. It wasn't only girls of nineteen and middle-aged men who lost their heads and hearts. It could happen to anyone.

CHAPTER SEVEN

THEY arrived at the airport to find the flight to Phuket delayed.

Had she been travelling alone—although in that case she would have saved money going south by bus or train—Clary would have had to wait on a plastic chair in the main concourse or in similar noisy discomfort in the tourist departure lounge. Instead of which, when they had checked in, Alistair sent them upstairs to the Royal VIP lounge.

'I'll join you in a few minutes,' he said.

A ground stewardess in the fuchsia suit and striped blouse of Thai Airways welcomed them to the lounge provided for first-class passengers. Here there was a free bar service, orchids on glass-topped tables and an international selection of newspapers and magazines.

It was the first time Clary had seen a *Financial Times* since parting from Miles, but the reminder of their life together no longer caused her either pain or chagrin. Strangely, losing her temper with Alistair at Wat Phra That seemed to have released a lot of repressed emotion and left her feeling spiritually cleansed.

While the stewardess was making coffee for them, Clary said to Nina, 'Although this is very comfortable, it would really have made more sense for us to say goodbye to Alistair at the Oriental instead of him coming with us and having to kick his heels here after we've gone.'

That way saying goodbye to him would be over instead of to come, she thought.

'Maybe by the time we take off he won't have all that long to wait for his flight. Once they start, these delays can drag on,' said Nina, a more experienced air-traveller.

Miles had had a phobia about flying, so Clary's holidays with him and been spent in places they could get to by car. Her first long journey by air had been the flight from London to Djakarta where she had started her travels in Indonesia.

But Nina had regularly jetted across the Atlantic from her expensive boarding school in England and her finishing school in Switzerland to spend holidays with her mother in places like Newport, Rhode Island, and Palm Beach, Florida. Although, from what Clary gathered, she had not been a welcome visitor but had had to keep out of the way when the men she referred to as 'Aileen's boyfriends' were around. And since leaving the finishing school she seemed to have been left to fend for herself.

'*Time* . . . *Newsweek* . . . What a boring lot of magazines!' the younger girl said, twirling the stand on which the papers and periodicals were arranged. 'I'm going down to see if there's anything better at the bookstall.'

Not long after her departure Alistair appeared. Either he had come up the stairs and Nina had used the lift, or vice versa, because he said, 'Where's Nina?'

Clary explained, causing him to say curtly, 'It would do that girl good to have nothing but *Newsweek* to read for six months. Her knowledge of world affairs is abysmal. Considering the money spent on her education, she seems barely literate . . . quite incapable of earning her living if she didn't have funds from the trust her mother persuaded my father to set up for her. Would you like a drink to follow that cup of coffee?'

'No, thanks . . . not at the moment.'

'I'll have a whisky and soda.' He went to the bar.

When he came back and sat down, he said casually, 'By the way, I'm coming with you.'

Clary's heart gave a violent lurch. 'C-coming with us?' she stammered.

'Yes . . . you don't mind, I hope?'

Minding didn't express the turmoil of conflicting feelings she was experiencing inwardly.

'But how *can* you come with us?' she demanded. 'What about your flight to London?'

'I've had it changed,' he told her, in the same casual tone with which he had knocked her sideways. 'I've decided it's time I had a holiday and Koh Phi Phi sounds the perfect place to relax for a couple of weeks. It's years since I did any snorkelling . . . not since I was in my twenties.'

Still trying to decide which was her predominant reaction, delight or dismay, Clary said, 'But in that case you don't need me around. You can keep an eye on Nina yourself.'

'On the contrary, your presence is essential. You're needed on three counts: to be an improving influence on her, to be a buffer between us, and to make it all *comme il faut*, which it certainly wouldn't be if she and I were there on our own. I don't want anyone thinking I've a teenage popsie in tow. If you're there they won't.'

'Why come with us at all? Why not go somewhere else where you won't be irritated by the things about Nina which annoy you?' she suggested.

'Because I like the sound of Koh Phi Phi...and also I like your company. Holiday pleasures are more enjoyable shared. Are you trying, without actually saying it, to tell me that you would rather I went somewhere else, Clary?'

'Why should I do that? I—I like your company too.'

He lifted a quizzical eyebrow. 'You do?'

At this point, to Clary's relief, Nina came back. Nevertheless it annoyed her when the younger girl's response to Alistair's change of plan was noticeably unenthusiastic. Clearly she was already taking her release from prison completely for granted.

It was almost nine when they boarded. Flying time to Phuket was sixty-five minutes, and soon after take-off the cabin crew began to lay the fold-down tables with crisply laundered purple and lilac damask cloths and lilac linen napkins.

By the time they'd had brandy with their coffee, Clary could feel the plane beginning to lose height. Soon the wheels were thumping on the runway and her second luxurious flight under Alistair's aegis was over.

At the entrance to the airport, a driver was holding a placard with 'Pearl Village' written on it. Soon they were in a minibus on the way to their night stop.

The teak-raftered lobby where Alistair registered and the two girls also signed their names was open to the night on both sides. A refreshing breeze was fluttering the pearl-disc tails of three ornate chandeliers, making them tinkle softly. As they were led to their rooms by a long covered walkway, they had glimpses of a tropical garden, palms decorated with fairy lights, a floodlit pool with a waterfall and waiters clearing the tables where people had been having dinner on a terrace under the stars.

Their rooms were next to each other with mother-of-pearl numbers on the doors. Clary was putting her sponge bag in the bathroom when there was a tap at the door and a bell-boy delivered a bowl of fruit wrapped in Cellophane.

She was peeling a tangerine from a selection which included a pineapple, a papaya, a banana and a large piece of water-melon, when there was another knock at the door.

This time it was Alistair with a bottle in his hand.

'How about some champagne to wind up the day?'

'That would be lovely,' she said, standing back to let him come in. When he had stepped past her, she put her head out of the door. 'Is Nina going to join us?'

'I haven't suggested it to her. Do you feel I should?'

Oh, dear, she thought, ball in my court.

'I think she'd feel rather hurt at being left out, don't you? I'll knock on her door.'

As she walked the short distance to Nina's room, she was almost certain she heard him say mockingly, 'Coward!'

She woke up early, as usual, and made herself a cup of tea with her miniature immersion heater hooked over the rim of a plastic mug, two essential items of backpacking equipment, in her opinion.

Taking the mug and the second tangerine on to the small veranda outside her room, she sat down to wait until seven when she could swim in the pool.

Birds were singing and a girl gardener was watering the grass. One or two hotel guests were exploring the extensive grounds. Suddenly, on a path at the far end of the garden, a tall figure appeared, with a towel over his shoulder. He must be heading for the beach.

Clary watched him until he disappeared from view, wondering what if anything would have happened if they had drunk last night's champagne *à deux* instead of with Nina present.

Would he have stayed talking longer? Would he have kissed her goodnight? What *were* his intentions towards her? Perhaps he had none; or perhaps when he made that remark about shared pleasures being more enjoyable, it had been in his mind to persuade her to share some more intimate recreations than swimming and snorkelling.

She wished she knew what to make of him. Was he still single because he didn't want or need to commit himself to any one woman? Or was he, in spite of his good looks, rather a lonely man who had never met a woman he could love?

Alistair had suggested meeting for breakfast in the central clubhouse at a quarter to eight. Clary was there on time, her appetite sharpened by a vigorous swim in the pool. She had called Nina, on her way to and back from the pool, but the younger girl was six minutes late arriving, causing Alistair to look at his watch and say, 'What kept you?'

'Oh, God! Does it honestly matter? I only want coffee anyway,' she said, with a glance of revulsion at Clary's Thai breakfast, a rice and shrimp broth, and Alistair's fried eggs and bacon. 'Spare me the nag about punctuality, and I won't tell you what that stuff is doing to your cholesterol level.'

'Amazing! She's heard of cholesterol. I wonder if she can spell it,' he said, when Nina had passed on in the direction of the lavish buffet.

Clary laughed. 'Probably not, but you have to admit that she's right. That's not a very healthy breakfast.'

'But I had a run on the beach as well as a swim. I keep in pretty good shape,' he said, putting another forkful of bacon and egg into his mouth.

Clary had seen what good shape he was in on the pool deck at the Mae Ping. There was nothing out of condition about Alistair's body. To her he appeared to have the muscle tone of a professional athlete.

'You said you were your father's principal heir. Are you now the head of his engineering business?' she asked.

'Among other things. I've been able to expand and diversify. Linco is now a much larger, more complex corporation than it was when he died, but even so my expansion doesn't match his achievement. It's starting from nothing and making the first million which is hard. After that it's comparatively easy.'

'You're the chairman of Linco?' she exclaimed.

Alistair nodded. 'I take it you've heard of us?'

'Who hasn't? You're a household name.'

'Only in upmarket households. We don't have the corporate charisma of Virgin or Lonrho. I doubt if Linco means much to the tabloid readership.'

'Probably not, but I shouldn't think that bothers you. How slow of me not to connect Lincoln with Linco . . . especially when I've actually worked for one of your subsidiaries.'

'Really? How come?'

'My job was conference production. When Lincompute launched their first line of personal computers, I helped to organise the conference to convince the sales staff that their product was the best.'

'You must have done a good job. The launch went off even better than I anticipated and we're still giving Alan Sugar, the man behind the main rival firm, his most serious competition.'

'Yes, as I don't think your product really is significantly better than his, I feel we did do a good job,' Clary agreed. 'It was the success of that conference which swung my promotion from production assistant to producer. But a couple of years after that the company merged with another and in the subsequent reshuffle my post went down the drain.'

'Which was when you decided to chuck the rat-race and travel?'

As Clary nodded, Nina came back and asked, 'What time are we moving out? I'd like to have a swim in that fabulous pool.'

'Sorry, there won't be time,' said Alistair. 'You should have swum before breakfast like Clary and I did.'

'Oh, shit!' Nina said crossly.

He looked disapproving. Having finished his breakfast, he asked them to excuse him and strode away to the staircase leading to the lobby.

'I suppose Saint Alistair never says rude words,' Nina muttered sarcastically, glowering at his broad back.

'Not in front of women, I imagine.' Clary watched him mount the stairs. 'I think you only said it to annoy him. Why not try to please him, Nina? He's come halfway round the world to help you. You owe him a lot, and not just money. Without him, you'd still be locked up.'

'I know. I am grateful really,' Nina admitted. 'But I feel he despises me and it puts my back up. I'm not that bad, am I, Clary? He makes me feel like some kind of half-witted tart. Is that how you see me?'

Clary met Nina's greeny-gold eyes with their half defiant, half appealing expression.

'I think you have terrific potential, but you haven't quite got it together.'

Look who's talking, she thought.

To her astonishment, Nina said, 'I know, but you have. I recognise style when I see it. You never wear anything fancy, but you always look great. You don't have split ends and split nails. You know the right way to behave in every situation. OK, so you're backpacking now, but yesterday at the Oriental they treated you the same way they treated Alistair. Respectfully. They looked at me like something the cat had dragged in.'

'You imagined it, Nina. The staff there are so well trained they wouldn't look at anyone like that—except perhaps a rowdy drunk, and even that situation they'd deal with tactfully. But since you're asking my advice, I think it's really more chic, especially in this climate, not to wear very much make-up. You have wonderful eyes which don't need mascara and liner, especially not on an island.'

She glanced at her watch. 'If you've finished your coffee, I think we should collect our things. Hey, you haven't drunk your water. I used not to drink with meals, but I do here. When I first got to Indonesia, I didn't realise how important it was to drink several pints a day, and I got slightly dehydrated. It makes you feel rotten.'

Twenty minutes later, in another minibus, they set out for Phuket Town at the southern end of the largest of Thailand's islands. It was not a long run on a good road through interesting scenery with a glimpse, in passing, of the monument to the two women who rallied the Thais to beat back invading Burmese in 1785.

The bus dropped them at the Pearl Hotel in the centre of town where they left their baggage under the bell-captain's eye while Alistair went in search of snorkelling equipment and the two girls looked round the nearby Ocean department store.

When Clary had suggested that, if Koh Phi Phi was a mecca for snorkellers, he could probably rent a mask and flippers there, he had said, 'I'd rather use my own gear. What about you two? Are you going to snorkel with me?'

Nina had tried and disliked snorkelling. The mask made her feel claustrophobic. Clary would have liked to try it, but had several reasons for pretending she wasn't keen. She didn't want to spend her money on equipment which would become an encumbrance when her time at Phi Phi was over. She certainly didn't want Alistair to pay for it, as he might insist on doing. And she didn't want to spend more time in his company—even face down in the sea—than was unavoidable.

When she and Nina returned to the hotel a few minutes before the time Alistair had specified, he was already there but no longer wearing the clothes he had had on before. Now he was dressed in the style of a backpacker with one of the imitation Lacoste shirts which were on sale everywhere at a fraction of the cost of the genuine article, and a pair of cheap cotton trousers with a drawstring waist, several patch pockets on the legs and a large fake Benetton label stitched down the side seam.

'Wow...get you!' Nina exclaimed.

Alistair grinned. 'When in Rome...'

The grin formed engaging creases in his lean cheeks and showed off his excellent teeth. It also made him look younger and more relaxed.

Clary found herself thinking how much better it would be if, instead of being the head of Linco and in the same league as Richard Branson, Tiny Rowland, Terence Conran and other high-flying entrepreneurs, he were an ordinary man who, as he'd said of her, had 'dropped out of the rat-race' to see the world and its wonders from a backpacker's perspective.

She put the thought from her at once. That sort of wishful thinking had to be stamped on immediately.

A sea eagle was flying in slow circles over the river mouth as the ferry to Phi Phi Island chugged slowly past the docks where Phuket's large fishing fleet was berthed.

After watching the bird through his binoculars, Alistair offered them to Clary, giving her a close-up of the eagle's cinnamon plumage and predatory head.

They were sitting on a bench at the stern. Nina had climbed a ladder to reach the area on top of the ferry's interior accommodation. There was nobody sitting inside, but several young people were settling themselves and their belongings on the top deck and Nina was preparing to sunbathe.

'Splendid birds...eagles,' said Alistair, taking another look at it after she had handed back his glasses.

'Where do you watch birds in England?' she asked.

'I have a weekend cottage on the north coast of Norfolk. I used to drive down once a month to get some fresh air in my lungs. Now I go twice a month by helicopter...saves time. The roads to that part of the country are better than they were, but I prefer flying to driving.'

'Do you fly it yourself?'

He nodded. 'And I've more than recouped the time it took me to learn in time saved since I qualified. Time is important to me. I hate to waste it sitting in traffic snarl-ups or driving on roads which demand concentration I'd rather be applying to other things.'

'Why not have someone to drive you?'

The suggestion seemed to amuse him. 'A chauffeur-driven Rolls-Royce with a cocktail bar and a tele-phone? My father had one of those, a Silver Shadow. It symbolised his achievement. He revelled in riding around "like a nabob", as he put it. But I didn't have his struggle from rags to riches. A stately car with a driver would make me feel middle-aged, and the playboy image which goes with a Ferrari doesn't fit either. Not that I have or want a public image anyway.'

'Now I come to think of it, I did hear people talking about you—the great driving force behind Linco—when I was helping to set up that conference,' said Clary. 'But I suppose if you hear a name but there's no face to go with it, you tend to forget it.'

'That's right...that's why manufacturers advertise. If they didn't, the public would quickly forget about their products. It's exactly the same with showbiz people. Without constant publicity they soon slide into oblivion.'

They were on the open water now, heading south on the Andaman Sea on a two-hour voyage to the two specks on the map known jointly as Koh Phi Phi; Phi Phi Don being their destination and Phi Phi Leh a neighbouring island inhabited only by sea swallows whose nests were collected to become an expensive soup in Chinese restaurants.

Now that they were at sea Alistair pulled off his shirt.

'Would you mind oiling my back?' he asked.

From a zipped pocket at one end of his newly acquired large roll-bag which now held his original luggage as well as today's acquisitions, he produced a container of factor six sun lotion.

'I don't burn easily,' he said, as he handed it to her. 'But at this time of day, and on water, it's best to play safe.'

There was no way Clary could refuse to do what he asked, but she wasn't happy about it. Instinctively she shrank from touching him.

'What's the matter? Can't you get the top off?' he asked, looking over his shoulder a few moments later.

'Yes, yes…no problem,' she said quickly, the delay being caused by her reluctance, not by a technical hitch.

Turning the plastic bottle upside down, she squeezed a squiggle of cream between the tops of her shoulder blades, then transferred the bottle to her left hand in order to spread the cream with her right hand.

After the first tentative touch the feel of his skin reminded her of the texture of the expensive hide bag she still had in store at her parents' house. No, it was softer than hide, more like a taut chamois leather.

Against her will, she was aware of the same tactile pleasure she received from stroking a cat or resting her palms on sun-warmed stone or cool marble. But this pleasure was subtly different because this was a man she was touching, a man whose excitingly strong and virile body had already delighted her eyes and now made her hand long to linger, to stroke, to caress.

Instead of which she applied the sun cream as lightly and quickly as possible, trying to detach her mind from the sensual enjoyment felt by her fingers; trying to ignore the tremors going on deep inside her, tremors she had felt before, but never as powerfully as now.

CHAPTER EIGHT

CLARY'S first impression of the island where she was committed to spending the next two weeks—an arrangement she was regretting more and more strongly!—was that it wasn't as remote and quiet as she had hoped.

Indeed, in the vicinity of the jetty where the ferry put them ashore, it seemed to be quite a bustling place, with cafés and food stalls and even a police station.

That the only person on the station's veranda was a man in civilian clothes having a snooze in a deck chair was reassuring. Even so, there were far more people about than she had expected. She could only hope a lot of them were day-trippers from Phuket who would leave Koh Phi Phi before sunset.

They had been met at the jetty by a youth with a luggage cart from Ton Sai Village, the cottage colony where they had reservations.

Another unwelcome surprise, as they followed him along the dirt path which skirted the long crescent beach, was the sight of foreign girls sunbathing with bare breasts. Clary had hoped this European habit, so offensive to the modest Thais, would not have permeated here. But it seemed that, like the sailors and colonists of earlier centuries, the majority of modern tourists weren't interested in the manners and mores of the indigenous people. Coming first for wealth and now for pleasure, Westerners were still a corrupting influence, and it made her feel ashamed to be a tourist, even though she herself tried always to behave with respect and courtesy.

Unlike the rooms they had occupied last night, their huts here were not together. But all were along the front row of huts, with the sea only yards from their verandas.

'We'll have "happy hour" at my place. Hut Five at five o'clock,' said Alistair, before they separated to unpack and settle in.

Each hut consisted of a narrow veranda with two wooden armchairs, a fairly spacious twin bedroom with two more comfortable cane chairs and a bathroom at the back. There was no bath, only a shower draining into a hole in a corner of the blue-tiled floor.

But even if the accommodation was far below the level of the Mae Ping and not to be compared with the Oriental, it was still good by Clary's standards, and to be so close to the ocean was wonderful. If the tide had been in she would have made a bathe her first priority, for it was some time since she had swum in the sea and she'd missed it.

Instead she unpacked her shampoo, unwrapped the little cake of soap on the hand basin, then stripped off to have a shower.

There was no hot tap here, but she was accustomed to that. In a climate like this, who needed hot water? Unless Alistair did, for shaving. With more foresight she could have tried to buy him a mini immersion heater in town this morning. Perhaps he would arrange for hot water for shaving to be brought to his room, or maybe he used an electric razor.

A mental vision of Alistair standing in his bathroom, having to stoop to get his head and shoulders under the nose of the shower, revived the disturbing feelings induced by touching him on the boat. This was followed by another vision of him in *this* bathroom with her, his long hands caressing her body while she lathered her hair.

A knock on the outer door made her jump and swear under her breath. Her head now capped with thick foam, she rinsed off her hands, wrapped a towel around herself sarong-fashion and pattered to her bedroom door.

'Who is it?'

'It's me.' The voice was Nina's.

Clary opened the door.

'Oh, sorry... you're having a shower. I'll go to Alistair.'

'He may be in the shower too. What's your problem?'

'The lights in my room aren't working,' said Nina. 'Neither is the air-conditioning.'

'Did you activate your power supply by putting the tag on your room key inside this box on the wall?'

'No, I didn't. As it isn't a punched-card key like we had for the rooms last night, I didn't realise I had to.'

'It's the same system but less swish. Sometimes with this kind of tag you have to put a wedge down as well. My tag is a loose fit, so I've wedged it in place with the key.' As Clary showed Nina how, she felt a glob of lather beginning to slide down her neck.

When she returned to the bathroom, she made a determined effort not to allow the thoughts which the younger girl had interrupted to come back into her mind. But it was difficult. Rubbing sun cream on

Alistair seemed, like the tag with the power supply, to have activated her need to be loved.

For a long time that desire had been dormant. She had lived as chastely as a nun, all erotic feelings extinguished by the loss of her job and the ending of her life with Miles.

Now, all at once, those feelings had revived. She was suddenly longing to be kissed, to be held close.

Soon after sunrise next morning, Clary was watching a bird with yellow legs hopefully poking its yellow beak into a crab's hole, when Alistair's voice said, 'Good morning.'

She was sitting on the end of a white wooden lounger, placed sideways on to the sea. When she turned her head he came and sat beside her, standing his black rubber flippers against each other in an inverted V and resting the mask on top of them.

'How did you sleep?' he asked, after she had said good morning.

Until he appeared she had had the beach to herself, apart from a couple of youths desultorily sweeping the sand and picking up litter. That there should be any litter in such a beautiful place troubled Clary.

'Very well, thank you. And you?'

He nodded. 'The beds are good even if the bedside light isn't. Nor do I like the wire hangers in the wardrobe.'

'One can't have everything,' she said. 'I'd rather wake up to this——' her gesture encompassed the towering cliffs to their right, the calm crystal sea and one or two ocean-going yachts anchored out where the water was deep even at low tide '—than a cupboard full of good quality hangers. I agree with you

about wire ones, but are they worse than the kind
which can only be slotted on to the built-in rail?'

'Yes, those are a pest,' he agreed. 'And I wouldn't
have thought it was worth irritating the good guests
to defeat the baddies who steal traditional hangers.'
He rose. 'I'm going to take a look at the fish popu-
lation. Later on I thought I'd stroll round to the place
we saw lit up last night...see what they offer for
breakfast. Will you join me?'

'Why not?' Clary said, smiling.

As he picked up his gear and waded into the water,
she thought, You know damn well why not! You
should have refused...made some excuse not to go.

Then another voice in her head said, Oh, come on,
that's being silly. Breakfast *à deux* isn't like dinner *à
deux*. Where's the harm? Anyway, if you fancy him
and he fancies you, why not have a holiday romance?
Other girls do...other girls wouldn't hesitate.

Waist-deep in the clear sunlit sea, Alistair was
swilling salt water round the inside of his mask. Each
movement of his arms made a muscle move on his
back, reminding Clary how it had felt when she
touched it yesterday.

As she watched him fitting on the flippers before
striking out for deep water, the mental dialogue continued, one side of her nature debating with the other;
her libido putting forward specious arguments to persuade her intellect to be more laid-back, less prissy.

Alistair had moved fast in the pool at the Oriental,
but now, with his muscle-power assisted by the long
blades of the flippers, he seemed to shoot through the
water at, to echo his own phrase, a rate of knots. She
wished she were out there with him. Rising, she
stepped out of her thongs and walked into the water.

*   *   *

'You said your father had several younger brothers and sisters. Do you have much to do with them and their children?' Clary asked, as they walked past the spirit house of a larger holiday colony, Pee Pee Island Cabana. There was a glass of water and two little bowls of food on the platform in front of the spirit house, she noticed.

'No, unfortunately not,' said Alistair. 'Apart from his mother, who was proud of him, his family resented his success. Their jealousy didn't prevent them from accepting his generosity,' he added drily. 'It's the same with their children...my cousins as they would be if we were related by blood. Unfortunately they've been brought up with the same grudging outlook. I do what my father would have done for them, but there's no real family feeling. I shall always be an outsider which, in a way, I understand. How do you get on with your family?'

They were in the coconut grove now and he paused to take hold of a dead frond which had fallen across the dirt path. Watching him shift it to the side, Clary thought it was probably typical of him. Most people would have stepped over or round the once graceful but now dried-out frond. They wouldn't have bothered to clear the pathway for others. It wasn't their responsibility. But he, a rich man, a tycoon, had bothered, just as he had bothered about Nina when he might very easily have left her to stew in jail until her mother could be summoned. He would always do more than he needed to. It was one of the hallmarks of the special people, the outstanding people.

'We get on pretty well,' she said, in answer to his question. 'Ideally they would have liked a son first and then a daughter...a daughter who married young and provided them with several grandchildren.'

'You may yet do that,' he said. 'Do you like children?'

'I'm not sure that I do. I never could work up much interest in the babies of my school friends. The only ones I have felt an impulse to cuddle have been Asian babies. They have such appealing little faces and they don't seem to howl as much as ours do. *Oh*!'

The startled exclamation was in reaction to receiving a violent push. A fraction of a second later a large coconut landed with a thud on the path.

'Sorry to knock you about, but I happened to glance up and saw it start to break loose,' said Alistair, putting his arms round her. 'There was nothing I could do but shove you out of the way. Damned dangerous...dropping like that. All the palms lining paths should have the nuts removed before they get to that stage. A bash on the head from a large coconut could be serious.'

'If not fatal,' said Clary, more shaken by being in his arms than by narrowly missing being brained.

'Are you all right? Did I hurt you?'

He was holding her disturbingly close, one arm round her waist, his other hand gently rubbing the place where a buffet from the heel of his hand had sent her staggering sideways. 'I hope I haven't bruised you.'

'Better a bruise than another crack on the head,' she said unsteadily, not knowing how to extricate herself from this unexpected embrace.

The arm round her tightened.

'What a fool I am,' he said abruptly. 'That's why you don't want to snorkel...because your head is still sore. I expect it's hurting a lot more than you let on. Let's have a look.'

He took his arm from around her, but only so that his left hand could curve round her neck, turning and tilting her head in order that the fingers of his right hand could gently part her hair in search of the tissue damaged on the Stairway to Heaven.

'It's fine...just a little bit tender...nothing to speak of.'

Clary knew that her voice sounded breathless. Hardly surprising when her heart was pounding as if she'd just run half a mile.

'Yes, it's still badly discoloured. I bet it's as sore as hell. I can quite understand your not wanting the pressure of a strap there. Thoughtless of me to suggest it. But perhaps by next week you'll feel up to wearing a mask. It would be a shame to miss seeing the fish here. This morning I was surrounded by a shoal of those black and white striped fish we saw in the tanks in the lobby of the Pearl Hotel yesterday.'

As he talked, he allowed her head to resume its normal position, but he didn't take his hand from her neck and now his thumb was at the back of her ear, making a little stroking movement like the absent-minded caress one might give to a cat one was holding while thinking about something else.

Whether the caress was more deliberate than it seemed, and whether he knew what it did to her, she couldn't tell. But its effect was so catastrophic—sending quivers of excitement along every nerve in her body—that her mind boggled at what would happen if he ever made love to her.

At this point he dropped his hand and stepped away. Following his glance, Clary saw they were no longer the only people using that section of the pathway. Now a party of departing guests, led by the youth with the baggage cart, were coming towards them.

'I didn't much like the look of the black and white eel in that tank,' she said, as they began to walk on. 'It had very spectacular markings but a rather unfriendly face, didn't you think?' To her relief, her voice sounded fairly normal.

'I saw one of those as well, but he dodged out of my way. They probably aren't aggressive unless they feel threatened,' said Alistair.

This morning he was wearing a papaya-coloured fake Lacoste with a pair of sea-green cotton shorts, another holiday outfit he must have bought in town yesterday. She supposed he would have his laundry done for him. She had already rigged a line on her veranda and washed out yesterday's clothes in the bathroom basin. They wouldn't take long to dry and then she would press them with her small travelling iron.

The place where they had breakfast was on the other side of the fishermen's village at the far end of the bay from the colony where they were staying. The café had been built round a large tree and they sat at a table overlooking a small rocky cove. From here the huts where they were staying were hardly visible, screened by coconut palms and other low-growing trees along the beach. Behind rose the mountainous profile of the eastern end of the island, the greenery growing on the rugged grey peaks showing that plenty of rain must fall here during the monsoon.

Soon after they had ordered breakfast, an American at the next table started talking to Alistair. He had also had a girl with him, and the four-way conver-

sation which followed suited Clary much better than
a tête-à-tête.

On the way back through the village she and Alistair
both borrowed books from an establishment which
was a combination of an excursions agency and
lending library. After paying a hundred-*baht* deposit,
Clary chose a paperback for which the fee was only
twenty *baht* a week. Alistair took out two paper-
backs, a thriller and a travel book. Then they strolled
past the many small restaurants built side by side along
the beaten earth street.

'Better send a card to my secretary, I suppose,' he
said, stopping to look at postcards.

He bought half a dozen, making Clary wonder who
the other five were for. Girlfriends?

She bought three and some stamps which here, she
discovered, cost one *baht* more apiece than on the
mainland.

'Rather a swingeing surcharge,' Alistair said drily,
when she mentioned this. 'Clearly the islanders are
making tourism pay. Although it may be that the
people making the profits are in fact fast-buck main-
landers,' he added, when a path leading off to one
side gave them a view of primitive palm-thatched huts
with chickens scratching round them. It suggested that
not all the islanders were making money out of the
visitors to their once isolated paradise.

Nina had been for a swim and was reclining on a
lounger, when they returned to their end of the bay.
Later they all had lunch at the little Muslim restaurant, Armida, not far from the island's health
centre and first-aid post.

That evening Alistair again had a happy-hour
session on his veranda. As being on time wasn't im-

portant, Clary delayed going to his hut in the hope
that Nina would have arrived before her. But although
he had placed a bedroom chair alongside the pair of
veranda chairs, Alistair was alone when she joined
him.

It was low tide and he was leaning forward, with
his elbows on the veranda rail, watching a long-legged
wading bird pacing along in a few inches of water.
He gave the glasses to her while he went inside to fix
a drink for her.

Five minutes later there was still no sign of Nina
and the bird had disappeared. They were both sipping
Mekhong and sodas and Alistair was telling her that
the couple in the hut next to his had seen a flock of
monkeys at the cliff end of the beach, when a man
went by on the brick path immediately in front of the
line of verandas.

There had been people passing ever since Clary arrived. Some of them smiled and nodded, some of them
didn't. This man looked lost in thought and seemed
not to notice them, but there were things about him
which caused Alistair to break off what he was saying
about the monkeys and raise an eyebrow at Clary.
She knew what was in his mind, and, frowning
slightly, she said, 'If there's one thing I've learnt on
my travels, it's not to judge people by their hair or
their clothes. He may have long hair and be wearing
slightly way-out clothes, but it doesn't necessarily in-
dicate that he's any less masculine or less decent than
you are.'

Slightly to her surprise, Alistair didn't treat her re-
proof as a joke. He said, 'You're right, of course. All
the same, I'm damned if I can see why any man would
want to have long hair in this climate.'

'His hair was about the same length as mine. It's no hotter than short hair if it's tied back. Actually I agree with you. I think men's hair looks better shortish. But long hair that's clean and tidy is a harmless affectation, don't you think?'

At this point Nina arrived, her hair now reduced to a very short crop of the much darker hair which had been at the roots of her blonde mane.

'How do I look?' she asked. 'Better?'

The next morning, while Alistair was snorkelling and Clary was swimming, she saw the man with long hair come out of one of the beachfront huts at the cliffs end of the colony.

As it had been the night before, his hair was brushed back from his forehead and temples and tied at the nape of his neck. But instead of wearing an Indian shirt of fine white lawn with some white embroidery round the neckline, and a pair of Muslim trousers, as he had last night, today he was wearing beach shorts.

Holding his hand as he walked to the water's edge was a child of about four years old, a little girl. Her only clothing was a pair of inflated armlets.

Clary swam and floated and swam, enjoying the warmth of the water and the beauty and peace of her surroundings, a peace now and then disturbed by the engines of islanders' boats, some still used for fishing but many engaged in running the visitors back and forth to other beaches.

She had thought that the man with long hair might soon be joined by the little girl's mother, who might or might not be his wife. But no woman came out of the hut, and he and the child were still playing water games together when Clary waded ashore.

Accustomed to the friendly ways of backpackers, as she passed them she paused to say, 'Good morning. What a perfect morning. Where are you from?'

The man smiled at her and said, 'Hi.' He turned to the child. 'Say hello to the lady, Fifi.'

The little girl beamed, 'Hello.' She had the pale silver-gilt hair which rarely outlasts early childhood, and her eyes were deep blue, like Alistair's.

'We've come here from the Philippines. I'm Pete Albany and this is my daughter Fleurette...shortened to Fifi,' he said, rising from the shallow water in which he had been kneeling.

'I'm Clary Hatfield from England. Do you mean you've been travelling in the Philippines or that's where you live?' she asked.

'Travelling...we've been travelling two years...since my wife died. We used to live in France. My mother is French. My father was American, hence my accent. What part of England are you from?'

For the next ten minutes or so their conversation followed the usual pattern among travellers; first the brief details about themselves, then a general outline of when and why they had set out, followed by an exchange of more specific information on places they could recommend or would advise avoiding.

'I was put off going to the Philippines by the political troubles,' Clary said presently.

By now they were sitting side by side in the shallows while the child splashed contentedly nearby.

'I guess they'll always have those, or for a long while,' said Pete. 'The thing which bothered me there were the ferries. They have a lot more sinkings than get reported in the press. I once went to a police station about something I'd had stolen and they had forty

bodies laid out on the floor from a ferry disaster.
They're the cheap way to get from island to island,
but I wouldn't use those ferries if I couldn't swim
better than average...and I never took Fifi on one.
She stayed with friends when I was island-hopping.'

'Can I keep an eye on her for you while you have
a swim?' she offered.

'Would you? That would be kind. She won't be any
trouble. She's a good little kid.'

Pete was having a vigorous swim, and Clary was
drawing simple pictures in the sand with a stick when
Alistair came back.

'Who's your friend?' he asked, smiling.

'Mademoiselle Fifi. How was your snorkel?'

'Great.'

As he described the brilliantly coloured fish, the
vivid corals, she noticed how rapidly his own colour
was changing, already acquiring the fast easy tan allowed by his natural pigmentation.

Seeing him now, completely relaxed, full of *joie de
vivre*, she realised that, although he had claimed never
to suffer from jet lag, he hadn't been as carefree as
this when he arrived in Thailand. The pressures and
responsibilities of his position, even though he bore
them lightly, must weigh heavily on him sometimes.
But now, for as long as they were here, he was concentrating on enjoying himself.

Pete came out of the water. He was inches shorter
than Alistair but still a fit, well-built man.

'This is Fifi's father...Pete Albany...Alistair
Lincoln.'

Pete held out his hand. 'Glad to know you.'

Clary saw Alistair's manner change as he recog-
nised Pete as someone he'd seen before. As the men

gripped each other's hands, Pete was smiling but Alistair wasn't. He had on the face he would wear as Chairman of Linco; reserved, watchful, shrewd, judgemental.

CHAPTER NINE

'ARE you travelling together?' Pete asked Clary when, after a brief conversation, Alistair had walked off to his hut.

She shook her head, knowing that what he was asking was: are you partners?

'There are three of us. I'm here as a sort of chaperon to Nina, who's nineteen and a connection by marriage of Alistair's,' she explained. 'He and I met last week.'

This time last week I hadn't even spoken to him on the telephone, she thought with astonishment.

'I guess it's time we had breakfast.' Pete swung his small daughter high above his head to give her a ride on his shoulders back to their hut. 'Thanks for minding Fifi. See you around.'

Clary went back into the sea and had another swim. She liked Pete and his child and felt sorry for them. It annoyed her that Alistair had been unfriendly towards him. Polite, but unfriendly.

Pete had felt the hostile vibes and had thought they might signal: this woman is mine. Keep your distance. But since that was not the reason for Alistair's antagonism, she could only assume that because of Pete's hair and clothes he had classified him as a dropout and didn't want to know him.

She was a drop-out too and he didn't seem critical of her, but perhaps as she was a woman he didn't think it mattered. Also there was nothing overtly 'hippie' about her.

Half an hour later, stretched out on a lounger, she watched a party of middle-aged Japanese men loading scuba-diving equipment on to a boat which like all the island fishing boats had three lengths of coloured cloth tied round the neck of the long upward-curving prow. This one also had a garland of flowers.

The Japanese were all wearing black rubber wet-suits with weights attached to their waists and knives strapped to their legs. They bustled back and forth, giving each other what sounded like staccato instructions.

'Off to blow up a battleship, by the looks of it,' said Alistair, from behind her.

The remark made her laugh. It summed up perfectly the seriousness with which the divers were taking themselves and their expedition. She liked his quirky sense of humour.

But when he said, 'Coming for breakfast?' she shook her head.

'I don't think I will this morning. I had too much dinner last night, I'm not really hungry. I'll make myself another mug of tea.' She had told him about her water-heater.

He nodded. 'OK, see you later.'

When he came back, an hour later, Nina was with her.

'Your secret mission in Bangkok is secret no longer,' said Alistair.

When Clary looked blank, he handed her a copy of the *Bangkok Post* folded to show part of the Readers' Letters column.

The paper had printed her letter thanking whoever had given her the handkerchief on the Stairway to Heaven. It was followed by an editorial postscript saying that if the owner of the handkerchief would contact the newspaper, they would be sent a replacement supplied by Miss Hatfield.

'That was a lot of trouble to take. Most people wouldn't have bothered,' he said.

'Most people wouldn't have had the time and the opportunity,' she said, embarrassed by his praise.

While Nina was reading the letter, he said, 'I've arranged for a boat to pick me up here at noon. I'm told there's very good snorkelling at a beach round that corner.' He pointed towards the left-hand side of the bay. 'There's also a restaurant which does good chicken and rice. Would you girls like to come and have lunch there?'

Clary looked enquiringly at Nina, leaving the decision to her.

Nina said, 'Sure, why not?'

The boat was on time and the boatman brought it close to the beach so that they could sit on the gunwale and swing their legs inboard. The thwarts were bleached grey, all the oil dried out of the timber, by long exposure to the burning Thai sun.

They were over the deeper water where the tour boats anchored when Clary noticed a trickle of blood on Alistair's foot.

'It's nothing,' he said, when she pointed it out. He examined his foot for a splinter but couldn't find one.

It took about ten minutes to reach the straight half-mile stretch of sand called Long Beach. Here was another cottage colony, rather more basic than theirs, by the look of it. The people bathing and lying on the beach were younger than those staying at Ton Sai Village, and Nina perked up at the sight of several unattached men. From what she had been saying to Clary earlier, it was clear that her experience with Sean had not put her off the male sex as a whole.

Alistair wanted to snorkel before lunch and had been told that the best place was round a group of rocks sticking out of the water at the far end of the beach from the larger of the two restaurants. However, he asked the boatman to drop them off near their lunch place and he left his belongings with the girls and set off along the waterline, carrying only his mask and flippers.

About an hour later, Clary was sitting in the shade of one of the few trees, idly listening to the conversation of some people who also wanted to keep out of the sun at this hottest time of day, when she heard one of them say, 'Yeah, but it's a whole lot better up there at Shark Point than at this end. There are too many boats coming and going around these rocks.'

She said, 'Excuse my butting in, but is that the Shark Point you're talking about?'—waving her arm at the rocks where Alistair would be snorkelling.

'That's it,' the man confirmed.

'Why is it called Shark Point?'

'Because there are sharks up there. Not big like the one in *Jaws*...around this size.' He measured a length not far short of the span of his arms.

'And it's all right to snorkel there?' asked Clary, aghast.

'I guess so. I wouldn't myself—I'm a coward. But other people do.'

'They haven't lost any tourists yet,' said one of his companions.

'How do we know? It's not the sort of thing they'd advertise,' said another man.

Everyone laughed, except Clary. She was thinking of the blood on Alistair's foot . . . of something she had read about scuba divers being killed by sharks only when there was blood in the water, a scent they could pick up from a long way away, a scent which excited them and made them aggressive.

If a man was swimming at a place where sharks were known to congregate, how much blood would it take to attract their attention? And surely even a small shark could take off a hand or a foot?

Acting on instinct, she jumped to her feet and ran down the beach to a boat which minutes ago had dropped off a couple of backpackers. Scrambling aboard, she made signs that she wanted the boatman to take her to Shark Point—fast!

'Hey, Clary . . . where are you going?' Nina, who was bathing, yelled to her.

'To tell Alistair something!' she yelled back. There was no point in panicking Nina.

Zooming over the clear green water, exhilarating on the trip here, was no joyride now. The length of the beach seemed miles, the speed of the boat far too slow.

At first she couldn't see any snorkels sticking up from the sea around the rocks. Then, as they came closer, several swimmers raised their heads, turning masked faces towards the approaching boat. None of them was Alistair.

He was on the far side of the rocks. At the same moment that she spotted him, he lifted his head, saw who was in the boat and waved to her. Clary turned to the boatman and indicated that she had found who she was seeking.

As he cut the engine, letting the boat glide towards the man in the water, she called out, 'Please get in the boat, Alistair. It's important.'

To her infinite relief, he didn't argue. His mask already pushed up on to his hair, he grasped the side of the boat and the muscles bunched under his wet brown skin as he swung himself up and inboard, making the boat rock violently from side to side.

'What's up?' he asked.

She couldn't answer for a moment. She felt sick with relief that he was out of the sea, intact, unhurt. All the way from the beach, she had been having visions...horrible, terrifying visions.

Forcing herself to speak quietly and calmly, she said, 'There are known to be sharks around these rocks. I don't think it's safe to swim here with an injured foot.'

'An injured foot?' he repeated. 'Oh, you mean that scratch on the way here. That was nothing, Clary. It stopped bleeding ages ago. I know there are sharks here—I've seen a couple. They're quite small...not dangerous. I'd already been told about them. I didn't mention them to you and Nina in case it made you nervous of swimming. They're not every-where...just around here.'

Clary said nothing. She was afraid she was going to be sick. It must be the result of having her stomach clenched tight with fear for what had seemed like an hour but had probably been about five or six minutes.

'But I've been longer than I intended, so I'll come back now,' he went on. 'I'm sorry you were worried about me. You had no need to be.'

'It was mainly because your foot had been bleeding.'

She watched him remove his flippers. She still felt queasy and shaky. The last time she had felt like this was after the shock of being told, if she couldn't pay her way, Miles had no further use for her. Now she had had another shock; different but no less traumatic. Because, a few minutes ago, when Alistair had seemed to be in danger, she had discovered that she loved him.

'What was all that about?' asked Nina, standing in the shallows close to the point where the boat nudged against the sand. 'What could you possibly need to tell Alistair that couldn't wait till he came back?'

Before Clary could answer, he said, 'Got some money on you, Nina? If not, run up and get some. Ten *baht* should do it.'

'Here you are, Nina, have this.' A tall, lanky boy in cut-offs with short spiky fair hair had joined her and was offering her a crumpled Thai note.

'Thanks, Joey.' She flashed him a smile before passing the note to Alistair to give to the boatman. When he and Clary had joined them on the sand, she said, 'This is Joey Brentwood from Australia. Joey, these are the friends I told you about ... Alistair and Clary.'

After shaking hands and saying, 'Hello, Clary,' Joey turned to Alistair with a mannerly, 'How do you do, sir?'

Clary, remembering some of the beer-swilling, loud-mouthed young Aussies encountered at Kuta, the surfers' mecca in Bali, was pleasantly surprised.

So, it seemed, was Alistair. He said, 'We're going to have some lunch now. Will you join us, Joey?'

'Thank you, I'd like to.'

'Fine. Then why don't you and Nina organise a table and Clary and I will be there in a few minutes.'

Clary had only to pull a hip-length cotton top over her dry swimsuit and run a comb through her hair to be ready for lunch.

While Alistair rubbed a towel over his wet head, he said, 'I hope you don't mind my inviting that lad to join us.'

'Of course not...it was a good idea. It's natural for Nina to want company of her own age. At first sight, Joey doesn't strike me as being another Sean, but asking him to lunch will give you more time to weigh him up.'

'That's what I thought.' Alistair gave his tousled hair a few casual flicks with a comb.

An immaculate comb, she noticed approvingly. One of the things she could have flung back at Miles when he was listing her faults on that last awful day had been that when he washed his hair he didn't scrub his comb.

After living with him for a while, she had taken to scrubbing it for him, and replacing his toothbrush when he needed a new one. Maybe his doting mother had been to blame for not training him to do those things for himself. But Clary, although never aggressively feminist, had felt strongly that it wasn't the duty of wives or girlfriends to nanny their men in those small ways—or to have to nag them to do things.

She had made up her mind that whenever—if ever—she became involved with another ·man, she would make sure his personal habits were not going to be a perpetual irritant to her.

Now here she was in love again—if, in fact, she had really loved Miles, which now she was inclined to doubt—and she didn't know the first thing about Alistair's bathroom habits. But somehow she couldn't imagine him leaving the bathmat soggy, the towels in a mess or, if he lived with a woman, the lavatory seat up.

'Right: shall we go?'

While her thoughts had been drifting back and forth between past and present, he had changed his wet trunks and pulled on a cotton-knit shirt. There was no dress code in operation at any of the island's beach cafés, but evidently he felt, as she did, that shirts for men and sarongs or tops for girls were more appropriate at meals, however informal, than bare chests and almost bare breasts.

The tables at the Paradise Pearl were thick slices of tree-trunk, varnished. Most of the lunchers were barefoot or wearing thongs and a good deal of sand had been carried up from the beach to scatter the cement floor. In front of the restaurant was a large tree with a monkey chained to it. People staying in the nearby huts stopped to play with it on their way to and from the restaurant.

Nina and her new friend were studying the menu when the others joined them. Joey jumped up and pulled out a chair for Clary. He waited for them both to be seated before he sat down again. The T-shirt which had been pulled through the back of his belt when they met him was now on. It had '...the answer is blowing in the wind' printed across the chest.

When they had ordered, Alistair said, 'Where are you from in Australia, Joey?'

'Canberra...at least, that's where my parents live now. I was born in Turkey and although I was at school in Australia, I was mostly abroad in the holidays...Italy...America...all over.'

'It sounds as if your father might have been a diplomat,' said Alistair.

Clary had been thinking the same thing.

'Yes, he was,' said the young Australian. 'He's retired now. There's an eight-year gap between me and my brothers and sisters. I was an afterthought,' he added, with a grin.

By the time they had eaten a chicken and cashew salad, it had emerged that his school had been Timbertops, where Prince Charles had spent time, and Joey was part of a stable and close-knit family whose standards he might have questioned at some stage of adolescence but now, at twenty, accepted.

They were waiting for their fruit salads to come when the man to whom Clary had spoken earlier, under the shade tree, came to their table and said to her, 'I think maybe I should apologise to you, miss.' He turned to Alistair. 'My friends and I were talking about Shark Point and your lady here overheard, and I think we gave her a real scare. We didn't mean to do that, but she was off and running before we could tell her that you weren't in any danger.'

'That's OK. Don't worry about it.' Alistair glanced at Clary. 'At least now I can be sure she's not hoping a shark *will* get me,' he said jokingly.

Everyone laughed, including Clary, who hoped the others hadn't noticed her blush when the man called her Alistair's lady.

Then the second course arrived, the man went away and, when Joey had answered Nina's question about sharks at Australian beaches, the conversation turned to surfing and Clary's embarrassment subsided.

'Seems the ideal playmate for Nina,' said Alistair later, when the two younger people had gone for a walk along the beach and he was swimming with Clary. 'Whether his family would feel the same way about him teaming up with a girl who's just been in jail is another matter. His mother certainly wouldn't take to her mother.'

'They're not likely to meet,' said Clary. 'Holiday friendships don't last, especially at their age. But I'm glad she's met somebody nice to have fun with . . . and to take the memory of Sean away.'

'I've been wondering what I would do if we ran into that swine,' said Alistair. 'Beat him to a pulp is the instinctive reaction, but I'm not a violent man, and would it reform him? I doubt it. Once a rat, always a rat.'

'In the long run, he may have done Nina a service,' she said thoughtfully. 'The worst experience of my life turned out——' She stopped short, regretting the unguarded reference to her past. 'Things which seem bad at the time can be all for the best in the end.'

'Sometimes, yes,' he agreed. 'Tell me about your worst experience?'

Short of snubbing him, which she didn't want to do, there was no way she could avoid answering the direct question.

After a pause, she asked him a question. 'Have you ever lived with anyone, Alistair...long-term, I mean?'

He said, 'Let's go and sit on those rocks, shall we? We shan't fry. The sun's not so hot now.'

The rocks at the end of the beach included large flat-topped slabs ideal for sunbathing.

'Watch out for sea-urchins,' he warned.

Clary wasn't too sure that a tête-à-tête on the rocks was a good idea. Then, as she swam towards them, she decided it could do no harm to tell him something about herself if, in exchange, she learned more about him.

Alistair gave her a hand to clamber on to the rocks; not because she needed it but because, like Joey, he had been raised to be chivalrous towards women.

When they were settled, he said, 'No, I've never lived with a woman, either long-term or short-term. You won't like this, I'm afraid, but I may as well be honest. The women in my life have all been other men's wives, either divorced or heading in that direction.'

He was right—she didn't like it. It pained her to think of him engaging in a succession of cold-sounding affairs.

'Why did you say "You won't like this"?' she asked.

'Because I think...I'm sure you're the sort of person for whom sex and love are concomitant. Therefore you're bound to disapprove of relationships in which love isn't an ingredient.'

'I don't know about disapproving. That suggests a "holier than thou" attitude which isn't attractive in people whose lives are models of perfection. Mine is anything but!' she said, with a rueful grimace.

He said, 'I'm certain it isn't a history of casual affairs...or of the considered affairs which I've had with women.'

'No, I haven't had either of those...just one long-term relationship which I thought was leading to marriage but wasn't.'

'What went wrong?'

'I lost my job, my salary, my ability to pay the household bills which were my share of a life in the so-called fast lane,' she said, with a shrug. 'Now, of course, I realise I'm a slow-lane person anyway. Basically what went wrong wasn't losing my job but not working out how *I* wanted to live in the first place...going along with ideas received from my parents, teachers, other girls.'

Alistair had been sitting with one long leg stretched out in front of him and the other drawn up as a rest for his elbow. The sun was no longer directly overhead but slightly behind them, moving in its slow arc from the visible horizon to the east to a horizon hidden by the island's mountainous hinterland.

It was as if he were sitting with a spotlight playing on his back, highlighting the sheen of his thick dark hair and giving his shoulders the tawny gleam of a glass of Bristol Cream sherry. Like his back, his chest was smooth except in the centre, between his flat dark brown nipples where there was a light dusting of hair, then none as far as his navel and down the flat hard-looking belly until, near the top of his bathing slip, it grew with a coarser texture, hinting at heathery curls hidden inside the brief dark red slip.

'And how do you want to live?' he asked.

Clary leaned back on her palms, watching the plume of spray shooting up like a white cockerel's tail feathers as a boat came zooming into view from around distant Shark Point.

She said slowly, 'I want to see and enjoy the whole world, not just the bit I was born in and those I might get to on holidays. I don't want to spend my life working for material possessions while my soul gradually shrivels. In the past year I've seen more and learnt more and *lived* more than in the five years before that. It's also cost amazingly little compared with my annual expenses when I was part of the rat-race. Somehow—and I haven't worked it out yet—I want to keep this new freedom.'

There was a long pause in which Alistair stared at the dancing lights on the sea, his eyes slits of brilliant blue between narrowed lids. She wondered what he was thinking.

At last he said, 'Perhaps if I had my life over again, I would choose the path that you're on…the freedom road. But it's too late for that. I can't chuck the life I'm in. Too many people depend on me for their jobs, their futures, their security. OK, so if I dropped dead as my father did, someone else would take over. But having taken on a responsibility I can't jack it in, however much I might like to.'

He sprang up. 'Time we were getting back.'

Clary thought he might hold out a hand to pull her to her feet. But he didn't. Without waiting for her to get up, he stepped lightly from rock to rock until he came to one from which he could dive into the sea.

She watched his long brown shape gliding upwards towards the surface. She had a strange feeling of regret and despair, as if she had held in her hand something irreplaceable which by an incautious movement she had dropped in the sea, never to be recovered.

CHAPTER TEN

AFTER dark the village street throbbed with taped music, voices and laughter from the ramshackle restaurants packed with an international crowd of young backpackers having a good time, and a sprinkling of adventurous older people.

Outside several restaurants there were large metal trays in which the proprietor's selection from the fishermen's catch was attractively arranged, with crabs, their claws securely taped, hanging from strings above.

In the kitchens at the back of the restaurants, male cooks in sweat-soaked singlets toiled over woks and barbecues, while in the half-darkness at the rear of the buildings women washed pans and plates.

Waiters and waitresses with a smattering of restaurant French, English, Italian and German bustled about serving Singha and Kloster beer, thick tuna steaks with fresh lime, shrimp and lemon grass soup, fried chicken with chillis, fish curry with noodles and much else.

That night they ate at the Kangaroo restaurant opposite the notice which read 'Collect Call Baht 50. Mama Is Waiting Your Phone Call'. Joey had dinner with them, having come over from Long Beach.

Soon after they had settled at a table for four, and Alistair had ordered beers for himself and Joey and pineapple shakes for the girls, Clary saw Pete Albany among the group of people inspecting the restaurant's fish tray.

He had told Clary that morning that it was easy to get baby-sitters for Fifi. The Thai girls who worked at Ton Sai Village were good with all small children and his daughter, with her blue eyes and silver-blonde hair, fascinated them.

Clary's instinct, seeing Pete on his own, was to say, 'Let's ask him to join us.' But her intuitive awareness that this wouldn't please Alistair made her keep silent and pretend not to notice Pete. The conflicting feelings made her uncomfortable. She knew it wasn't right to let her love for Alistair, which was never going to come to anything anyway, subordinate her wish to be friendly towards a man for whom she felt only compassion.

Before she could make up her mind what to do, Pete settled the matter by approaching their table and saying, 'Hi, there! Mind if I join you?'

'By all means.'

To her relief, Alistair's manner was less offhand than it had been at the beach. An observant waiter had already swung a vacant chair from another table into place at the end of the table between Clary and Nina.

'A beer, please,' Pete said to him. 'I've already picked out a steak from that *big* fish he's cutting up tonight,' he told the others, referring to the proprietor. 'I usually get here a little earlier than this when it's not so crowded. I hope I'm not intruding.'

'Not at all,' Alistair said civilly. 'Have you met Nina and Joey?' He introduced them.

It turned out that Pete's father had been an American diplomat and he and Joey had the same cosmopolitan background. The difference between them, apart from an age gap of ten years, was that Joey was having six months off before settling down to a career in journalism while Pete had chosen to give up his career as a lawyer.

'I really wanted to be a painter,' he explained. 'But, as my father said, you can't make a living at it, or not many people can. But now I have an income left to me by my late wife, and I also have a small daughter to care for, so trying to be a good painter makes more sense than being a nine-to-five lawyer and a weekend father.'

'Do you *like* looking after your little girl?' asked Nina, clearly feeling it wasn't a job for a man.

'I do,' he assured her, smiling. 'Fifi's no trouble at all. We get along fine. Both my mother and mother-in-law thought it was a crazy idea to bring her along on this trip, but I reckon she's as happy with me as she would be with either of them. I don't spoil her—I'm very firm. But I don't fuss over her either. If she has a fall or gets dirty, it's no big deal.'

'Are you painting here?' Clary asked.

'I'm doing a sequence of sketches to go with my travel diary. I hope it might make a book. Today I did a drawing of the guy in the hut next to mine.' Pete paused with a look of distaste. 'He's a big guy like you, Alistair, but not in the same shape as you are. This fellow is really gross. He's got a gut like an old bull walrus! I guess he's forty-five...fifty...and the little Thai girl he has with him is younger than Nina and built like a ballet dancer. Real petite and pretty, she is. It makes me sick to my stomach to see the two of them together and to know that he may have paid no more than two thousand *baht* to the *mamasan* who rented her to him.'

'Yes, it's revolting,' Clary agreed. 'When we came back from Long Beach she was in the sea by herself. She swims beautifully and looks like a mermaid with her long hair streaming down her back. I smiled at her and she gave me such a sweet smile back. I'm sure she's wretchedly lonely with no one to talk to and that hulk of a man making her put sun oil on his revolting flab as if she were his slave. Which she is, poor little wretch. Ugh! It doesn't bear thinking about.'

'If she doesn't like it, why doesn't she run away?' said Nina. 'She doesn't *have* to stay with him.'

'Where would she run to? How would she survive?' said Clary. 'This isn't Europe, with social security and welfare agencies to help people in trouble. She may have been sold by her parents because they were desperately poor. She's trapped, just as——' She stopped short, biting back the comparison which had been on the tip of her tongue.

But Nina guessed what she had almost said and looked as embarrassed and angry as if Clary had said it.

It was Alistair who continued smoothly, '. . . as half the world is trapped by poverty and illiteracy.'

Clary shot a grateful glance at him, but he appeared not to notice.

After dinner Joey paid for everyone to have a cone of coconut ice-cream from the stall near the corner of the street not far from the jetty and the bit of beach beside it where the water-taxis to Long Beach anchored.

He had decided that, if the Pee Pee Island Cabana colony had a vacant hut, he would move there the

following day. When they came to the Cabana reception area, Nina and Joey stopped off while the
other three strolled on to Ton Sai Village.

'It's too early to turn in. How about a nightcap on
the beach?' Pete suggested, as they passed their own
reception desk. 'If you'll each bring a glass, I'll bring
the liquor and the ice.'

'Good idea,' said Alistair.

Clary nodded agreement. It was far too beautiful
a night to be wasted reading in bed, particularly as,
for privacy's sake, the floor-length bedroom curtains
with their pattern of frigate birds had to be kept closed
after dark.

She went off to fetch a glass and also the loose
foam-filled squabs from one of the bedroom chairs.
These were used by everyone to make the unyielding
wooden beach beds more comfortable to lie on.

Alistair had already arranged three loungers in a
row facing the sea when she went outside.

Taking the squabs from her and placing them on
the middle of the three, he said, 'I'm sorry if I made
you feel like a slave the day before yesterday.'

'The day before yesterday?' she said blankly.

As she had already discovered on other islands, it
was easy to lose track of time on them. Only the daily
entry in her travel diary reminded her of the date, and
that only while she was actually noting down inci-
dents and sights she didn't want to forget.

'The day we came here,' he said. 'I more or less
forced you to sun-cream my back. I'm afraid it didn't
occur to me, until your remark during dinner, that
you might have found it objectionable.'

'You know I didn't,' she protested. 'There's a world
of difference between being *told* to do something and

asked to do it. I could have refused. The little Thai girl couldn't. I wouldn't put it past that man with her to hit her if she doesn't do as she's told. Also he's totally repulsive. You have——' As she had during the meal, she hesitated. But this time she finished the sentence. 'You have a very nice body which no one could object to touching.'

'Well, thank you kindly, Miss Clarissa,' he said, in a mock Southern accent. 'The same could be said of you, if I may be so bold. In fact I reckon there's quite a few gen'lemen hereabouts who'd jump at the chance to lay their hands on your body. Yessir.'

Because it was said in a strong Colonel Sanders drawl, she was able to laugh. But the thought that, unlikely as it seemed, Alistair found her body desirable sent a thrust of excitement through her.

Pete rejoined them, carrying a bottle and a tub of ice cubes. Brandishing the bottle, he said, 'This is only Mekhong, the local hard stuff. Is that OK for you guys?'

'It's fine for me,' said Clary. 'I always drink the local stuff, although with rather more caution since my experience in Bali. There I foolishly had some *arak* which didn't seem terribly potent while I was drinking it, but oh, boy, did I have a headache the following morning! Partly because I didn't have any bottled water in my hut to drink last thing. A woman I met there, a travel writer, told me that, especially in the tropics, it's important to end every day with a couple of glasses of water.'

'Yeah, that's good advice,' said Pete, as he splashed generous slugs of whisky into their tumblers and his own. 'I don't drink this stuff on a regular basis.

Mostly I stick to beer. How about you, Alistair? You don't look as if you pig out on anything.'

'Not very often,' said Alistair, leaning back on the lounger on Clary's left. He lifted his face to the sky. 'Look at those stars! If these beds weren't a bit short for me, I'd be tempted to sleep out here tonight.'

Clary looked up at the sky, alight with millions of stars, some as brilliant as pieces of diamanté scattered on the outermost of many layers of black silk chiffon, others the faintest glitter veiled by the unimaginable distance between them and this beautiful planet where she and the two men were star-gazing.

It wasn't beautiful everywhere—they had driven through parts of Bangkok which were terrible eyesores—but here, tonight, it was exquisite.

A soft warm breeze was rustling the palms. A cruise liner, strung with lights, was anchored far out where the ocean was many fathoms deep. Closer in, the riding and cabin lights of several yachts added their sparkle to the scene, as did the golden beads of light outlining the café where she and Alistair had breakfasted yesterday. But the most magical light was that of a huge full moon spreading a moon-glade on the calm surface of the sea.

And the full beauty of that was only revealed when Alistair fetched his field glasses through which, when he gave them to her, Clary saw amazing silver patterns shifting and glittering.

While she was looking at them, Pete went to check that his daughter was still asleep, the baby-sitter having departed when he came back from supper.

Handing the glasses back to Alistair, Clary said, 'Yes, it would be wonderful to sleep out here, but I don't think the security guard who patrol the place

during the night would approve. I notice that everywhere in Thailand—at all the more expensive places,
that is—the blankets on the beds are sandwiched
between two sheets. Why do you think that is?'

'To protect them on both sides, presumably. There
was a time—before dry-cleaning came in—when rich
people's blankets were always enclosed in blanket
covers the same way that duvets are put inside covers
now,' he told her. 'My mother was a maid in a large
private house when Dad met her. On the beds of the
family who employed her, the blankets had elaborate
lace-trimmed covers. Mum made her wedding dress
from parts of a blanket cover which had been badly
stained when the daughter of the house upset her
breakfast tray on it.'

Only a man with enormous self-confidence would
have revealed that bit of family history, thought Clary.
Many men in Alistair's position would play down their
humble origins, but he was too sure of himself to care
if some people though less of him because he had been
abandoned as a baby and later adopted by a couple
who had struggled up from poor beginnings.

'Did you ever see it?' she asked. 'Did your mother
keep it?'

'Yes, she was very sentimental. Even when Dad
could afford to buy her any ring she fancied, she preferred to go on wearing her original Woolworth's
wedding ring. Poor people didn't have engagement
rings, but he scraped up enough to buy her a cheap
eternity ring for their fifth anniversary and she went
on wearing that too—much to his annoyance.' Alistair
paused before adding, 'The wedding dress got thrown
out by Aileen.'

'Oh, no! Oh, how could she?' Clary exclaimed, horrified.

'With no trouble at all. When I came home for the holidays after Dad married her, the house was being redecorated and a lot of things I should have liked to keep had gone.'

'Without protest from your father?'

'Some protest, probably—I don't know. But a man in the grip of an intense infatuation is not in his right mind.'

Pete came back.

'Have you been up to the lookout point yet?' Alistair asked him.

'Not yet. I guess you'd need to start out at first light in order to get up there before the day hotted up. Oh, hi there, Nina. Have this lounger—I'll get another.'

'Please don't get up. I'm not staying,' said Nina, as the two men swung their feet to the ground, preparatory to standing up for her. 'Joey's got a room at the other place. I'm going to bed. Goodnight.'

'Just a minute, Nina,' said Alistair. 'We were discussing the lookout. If we go up early tomorrow, do you want to come?'

'How early?'

'Seven.'

She shook her head. 'Definitely not . . . unless Joey wants to go, and he won't be coming from Long Beach until about eleven. He's not an early bird either.'

'OK, we'll go without you. Will you join us, Pete? Your little girl couldn't walk it, but you and I could take turns carrying her if you think she'd enjoy it.'

'No, I'll join you, if that's all right? But I'll leave Fifi with one of the girls.'

Clary would have preferred to walk up to the island's highest accessible point alone with Alistair, but she made herself sound pleased to have Pete's company too.

They stayed talking in quiet voices until about eleven. Then the party broke up and they went to their huts, having agreed to meet at a quarter to seven.

Clary was in bed, reading, when someone tapped softly on the glass of the long windows on the veranda side of the hut. There was another small window at the back of the hut, but it looked on to the veranda of the hut behind and she kept the curtains drawn across it.

She had had a nightdress when she set out on her travels, but being washed out every day and dried in the sun had, in a year, reduced it to a faded rag. Since then she had slept naked with her sarong within reach in case of emergencies.

By now, she thought, Nina would be fast asleep. The tapper on the glass had to be Alistair or Pete. The only circumstances in which Pete would disturb her at this hour would be if his child were ill, and earlier he had reported that Fifi hadn't stirred since being put to bed.

That must mean it was Alistair out there. And, as with Pete, there could be only one reason why Alistair would want to see her at this time of night.

Shaking, she threw back the bedclothes, slid out of bed and reached for the sarong lying on the other twin bed. Her heart was fluttering like the wings of the birds on sale in the cafés at Chiang Mai and at the foot of the Stairway to Heaven.

But her mind was already made up. If Alistair wanted to make love to her, she would welcome him into her bed. For the first time in her life she was deeply, passionately in love, and although there might be no future in it, there was the present.

To survive the rest of her life, she had to make memories in the same way the Thais made merit.

CHAPTER ELEVEN

'NINA! What do *you* want?'

Clary knew that her disappointment must be audible and visible, but she couldn't hide the let-down she felt at finding it wasn't Alistair waiting to be admitted to her room.

'I must talk to you,' the younger girl said urgently. 'I knew you were still awake when I saw your light on.'

'If you knocked on every door where the light was on at this time of night you could find yourself seriously unwelcome,' Clary said drily, as the other girl stepped inside and she closed the door.

'Yes, but not here,' said Nina. 'You only met Pete this morning. You wouldn't be tucked up with him, and I can't see you tangling with Alistair.'

'As a matter of interest, why not?' Clary enquired.

'You haven't known him long enough. You're not the kind to go crazy over a man. Anyway, Pete's more your type. I can see you two shacking up when you've known each other a while. I think you'd suit each other. You wouldn't mind him being married before and having a daughter. I wouldn't want to take on someone else's kid.'

'Presumably you didn't come here to tell me that you thought Pete and I were ideally suited?' said Clary.

'No, I came to ask what you thought of Joey...what Alistair thinks of him?'

'He likes him . . . so do I. On the basis of what we know about him, I can't imagine anyone who wouldn't. He has very good manners. He's fun. His family sound nice. But don't go overboard about him, Nina. He's twenty, you're nineteen. You have more important things to do than fall in love with every nice boy you meet.'

Nina flung herself down in a chair. 'Such as?'

'Such as making something of yourself as an independent person before thinking about joining forces with anyone else. Who are you? What do you want out of life? What are you going to put *into* it? Look, could we discuss this tomorrow? I'm tired and I have to be up at six-thirty if not earlier.'

'I'm in love with Joey,' said Nina. 'OK, so we're both young. But I've had a lot of boyfriends and I'm sure he's had lots of girls. I just knew straight away that he was special, different from any of the others. I'm serious, Clary. It was love at first sight for me and I think it was the same for him.'

'It isn't long since you thought you were in love with Sean,' Clary reminded her.

'No, that was never love. He was exciting and sexy, but I always knew he was no good,' Nina admitted. 'The way I feel about Joey is totally different. I'm too excited to sleep. Could I borrow your mini-heater to make myself a cup of tea?'

'No, because I need it for the morning. But I'll make you a cup of hot chocolate—I have one sachet left from some I was given—and then you must go and let me get some rest.'

But long after Nina had gone back to her hut and Clary had put out the light, leaving the room illumined by the brilliant moonlight outside, she was unable to sleep.

She would have liked to swim, but soon after her arrival in the tropics someone had told her that it was unwise to swim at night because sometimes, during the hours of darkness, the largest and most voracious fish came closer to the beaches than they did during the day.

A loud thud outside reminded her of the coconut which might have hit her if Alistair hadn't shoved her out of the way. She remembered him stroking her, and the memory conjured up a vision of what she might be feeling now if it *had* been he who had tapped on the glass an hour ago.

Either she would be sleeping peacefully in his arms, or they would be making love for the second time. But perhaps if he had come, he would have found her a disappointment. During the final showdown, Miles had accused her of being cold and inhibited. Perhaps there was some truth in that. Their lovemaking had never been all that she had hoped ... all that she felt sure it would be for any woman Alistair made love to.

Fortunately she had set her alarm clock, otherwise she might not have woken with time to have a shower and a cup of tea before going to the rendezvous point, the restaurant near the entrance to the Ton Sai Village section of the beach.

She was punctual, but both men were there before her. They set off through the coconut grove at a brisker pace than would be comfortable later when the sun had risen.

At present the tide was out and water was still draining from the sloped part of the beach and running in glistening rivulets down channels in the wet sand. Further out the sea was the colour of steel, aluminium and platinum as the sun emerged from a bank of dove-grey clouds to the east. The humpy shape of the island far out on the right of the bay was clearer this morning, a sign that the air was less humid than usual.

To reach the lookout they had to walk halfway along the main street of the fishermen's village and then turn off to the left through the village proper; the village as it had been before the invasion of sun-seeking foreigners.

Most of the huts were built of natural materials, but it was clear that it wouldn't be long before these became obsolete, replaced by concrete blocks and sheets of corrugated iron with the 'instant slum' look they brought to every community where craftsmanship gave place to quick convenience.

On the far side of the village they passed through another colony of holiday huts, and here there was also a large public building for the showing of video films.

From ahead came the sound of saws and the shouts of workmen, and soon they were passing yet another holiday village.

'My God! In a year or two this island is going to be wall-to-wall tourism,' Pete exclaimed in dismay. 'We're lucky to be here now. Poor Fifi, what's the world going to be like by the time she's Nina's age?'

'Maybe by then the fast-buck-makers will be under better control and conservation will have replaced destruction,' said Alistair. 'But I wouldn't like to bet on it,' he added sardonically.

Clary had assumed that the way to the lookout would be a winding path which even the elderly could walk, at their own pace. It was an unpleasant surprise to discover that the next section of the route was a dry watercourse so steep that, in the rainy season, it must be virtually a waterfall. Although not completely perpendicular, it was certainly a seventy-degree incline; a climb, or at any rate a scramble, rather than a walk.

As she suffered from vertigo looking over a second-floor balcony, her instinct was to say, You fellows go ahead. I'll sit this one out.

Alone with Pete she would have confessed her dread of high places and steep ascents. But somehow with Alistair there she couldn't admit her weakness. Maybe if she gritted her teeth and didn't look down it would be all right. Deep down she knew that it wouldn't, but she persuaded herself that it would.

'Clary, are you all right?'

The question came from Pete when they were long past the point at which she dared look behind her.

Ahead of them Alistair was picking his way from rock to rock, as surefooted as a mountain goat, or a born climber.

'Yes...I'm fine,' she assured him.

But no one who didn't suffer from vertigo could know how far from the truth her answer was. Even without looking down she felt sick at the thought of the drop which was now below her, and sicker still at the thought of how much further there might be to go to the top of this stretch.

'You go on ahead . . . with Alistair. I'm out of condition . . . need a breather,' she said, flashing a forced smile at him.

'What's the hold-up?' Alistair called from higher up.

'Clary's out of breath . . . so am I,' Pete called back.

Suddenly, looking up at him, she didn't love Alistair. She almost hated him. It was *his* fault that she was up here. But for him, damn him, she would be safely on the ground, not insecurely poised a hundred feet up an ascent which might be nothing to someone with his perfect balance but was pure torture to her.

Beside her, Pete said, 'As a matter of fact I've a rotten head for heights. I didn't bargain for this.'

'Nor did I,' she admitted. 'Never mind: it can't be much further, and the view from the top will be marvellous.'

Somehow, knowing that Pete wasn't enjoying it either gave her the courage to go on. It must be much worse for him. Women were allowed to show fear, men who did lost far more face. If a woman showed courage that made her special, outstanding. A man was supposed to be courageous. Not to be was a disgrace.

It was that which got her to the top: wanting to help Pete to get there, not wanting to burden him with a nervous woman as well as his own stretched nerves.

At last the steep watercourse ended and the path became a gentle slope past a deserted hut which once had been someone's home but now was falling into ruin.

At the lookout, after a final scramble up and over huge boulders, they found Alistair chatting to a party of young Thais who had arrived there before them.

The view *was* superb. In spite of the terror she had felt on the way up, Clary was glad she had made it. From here it was possible to see how the island was formed: two mountainous areas linked by a narrow strip of flat land, on one side Ton Sai bay and on the other Loh Da Lum bay.

The young Thais were friendly, eager to practise their English and equally willing to demonstrate the tones which gave different meanings to words in their language.

Clary enjoyed the respite, trying to keep her mind off the descent. If she could have bartered a year of her life to be wafted by magic carpet back to the village, she would have done so. She knew it was stupid to be frightened, but she couldn't help it. The thought of going down turned her blood to ice-water. Going down, she would have to look down. There was no way to avoid seeing that horrendous drop.

For Alistair, going down was as easy as coming up. He might have been going down the Stairway to Heaven, so swift and easy was his descent ahead of them. Pete, too, seemed to find it easier on the way down. But for Clary it was much worse.

There came a point when the dizziness, the terror of falling became unbearable. She had to stop and sit down, closing her eyes to shut out the sight of the drop. The worst thing about vertigo was the feeling of being pulled into the void, like a pin being drawn to a magnet.

'Clary, what's wrong?'

It wasn't Pete's voice but Alistair's. A strong arm came round her waist, a firm hand closed over hers.

'You're as white as a sheet,' he said. 'My dear girl, why didn't you say you didn't like heights? I would never have dragged you up here if I'd guessed that.'

'I'm sorry... I know it's stupid.' She made herself open her eyes.

Alistair was beside her. Pete was standing on a rock below the one she was sitting on, the top half of his body blocking her view of the way down.

'You don't like it either, but you aren't making a to-do about it,' she said, mortified by the failure of her courage while he had the guts to stand there, not even holding on to anything.

'Neither are you,' he said kindly. 'As a matter of fact I was exaggerating. I thought it might help if you felt I had the same problem.'

'It did, but coming down is worse than going up,' she confessed, unable to repress a shudder at the thought of what lay behind him and the ordeal she couldn't escape because there was no alternative route.

'It would have been more to the point to make her turn back if you could see she wasn't happy,' Alistair said shortly. Then, in a milder tone, he went on, 'Don't worry, Clary. We'll go down very slowly and Pete and I will be below you all the way. You can't possibly fall with the two of us there to catch you. Hold on to me—come on now. You're going to be fine. In a few minutes' time we'll back in the village, having breakfast.'

At last they were at the bottom, and she gave a deep sigh of relief.

'Well done... now you can relax.' Alistair patted her shoulder.

'Thank you...thank you very much,' she said humbly.

But although he didn't let her see it, she knew he must think her a fool, and with justification. She could have spared herself all that humiliation simply by saying at the outset that she had no head for heights and would give the lookout a miss. Instead she had broken the rule she had made for herself after the break-up with Miles. Do *your* thing, not someone else's. Or, as Shakespeare had put it, more gracefully: 'To thine own self be true...thou canst not then be false to any man'. But she had been false to herself, trying to conceal a weakness from a man who seemed to have none.

And that was muddled thinking as well, she told herself crossly, as they walked back to the village, the two men discussing the extraordinary rock formations of these and other nearby islands.

Alistair must have his faults and weaknesses like the rest of the human race. Just because they hadn't emerged yet, it didn't mean they didn't exist. Falling in love with the man shouldn't blind her to his failings.

'I'm going to have a Thai breakfast,' he said presently, when they were sitting at a table in the restaurant where they had eaten the night before. 'What do you fancy, Clary?'

'I think I'll have scrambled eggs.'

'I'll have fried eggs and bacon,' said Pete.

The scrambled eggs turned out to be a rather leathery omelette chopped into strips. Looking at it, Clary realised that, still shaken from her recent experience, she wasn't very hungry. But she had been brought up to eat what was put in front of her, and in fact the eggs tasted better than they looked. After a few mouthfuls she began to feel better too. OK, so she had made an idiot of herself. So what? It wasn't the first time. It wouldn't be the last.

Later in the day, while Alistair was snorkelling, Nina was with Joey and Clary was reading on her veranda, Pete came along with Fifi.

'Hi, there. Is that a good book?'

'I think so. It's by an American writer whom I hadn't heard of before.' She held the paperback up to show him the cover. 'Have you read any of his books?'

Pete had, including the one she was reading. They discussed it for a few minutes while Fifi pottered about looking for things to put in the waste basket, inside a low picket fence, between Clary's semi-detached hut and the one on the far side of the passage leading to the rows of huts behind hers.

'Tidying up is her latest game,' said Pete, looking fondly at her.

'She looks awfully sweet in that outfit,' said Clary. The child was wearing a pair of clown's pants with shoulder-straps.

'Yeah, it's kinda cute,' Pete agreed. 'Marie-Fleur used to wear those baggy pants when she was pregnant. I want to explain something to you. When we were up on those big rocks at the lookout this morning, it reminded me of a place Marie-Fleur and I went on our honeymoon. I got to thinking about her and that's why, when we came down, I forgot you'd need some help. I'm sorry.'

'Oh, Pete . . . don't be. The whole thing was entirely my own silly fault.' After a pause, she said gently, 'Sometimes the past two years must seem like forever to you, and sometimes no time at all.'

He looked at her with some surprise. 'That's true. How do you know? Have you lost someone you loved?'

'No, not really. I was only guessing.'

'You guessed right—that's just how it is. Sometimes my life with my wife seems so long ago I can't even remember exactly how she looked. Other times the accident seems like yesterday. She was in an automobile smash...not killed...she died three days later.'

'Oh...poor girl...poor you,' Clary murmured, her throat tight with pity.

'I guess I'm over the worst now. But I really liked being married. I was never one of those guys who spend an hour in a bar on their way home from work, or weekends playing golf or whatever. I preferred staying home with my wife.'

'Perhaps in a few years' time, you'll marry again. I'm sure that's what Marie-Fleur would have wanted you to do.'

He nodded. 'If it had been the other way round I would have wanted her to find some nice guy and be happy again. Trouble is, there aren't many women the right age for me who haven't been married before. A widow would be fine, but I'm not so happy about taking on a divorcee. I never heard of a break-up where there weren't faults on both sides.'

'That's probably true,' Clary agreed. 'Not necessarily equal faults, but yes, even the "innocent" party must have made a bad error of judgement.'

'You've never been married, Clary?'

'I did live with someone for three years, but then we split up. That's why I started travelling. I've spent the past year on my own.'

'No romances along the way?'

She shook her head. 'No romances. Lots of pleasant acquaintances, but I've never been anywhere long enough to get serious.'

How long does it take? she was thinking. A fortnight ago I didn't know Alistair existed. I met him a week ago today. Now, if he wanted me, I would spend the rest of my life with him.

'I knew my wife from way back,' said Pete. 'Her grandfather was my mother's family doctor and whenever we went to stay with my French grandparents I'd see this cute little blonde with the blue bows in her hair. Fifi's going to look just like her when she gets a few years older. I sure hope I'm not still on my own when she gets to her teens. That's a time when a girl needs a woman to help her with dresses and make-up.'

'As a painter you must have a good eye for line and colour. That's all it takes...and good taste. I'm sure you have that. Did you choose the lemon clown's pants?'

They were still chatting half an hour later when Alistair came out of the sea. By this time Pete was sitting in the second chair on Clary's veranda with Fifi asleep on his lap, sucking her thumb, her long eyelashes like miniature feather fans.

To reach his hut from where he left the water, Alistair had to walk past them.

'How was it today?' Clary asked.

'Good.' With a nod, he passed on, not stopping to talk to them.

'Interesting guy, but not very communicative about himself. What does he do for a living?' Pete asked, when the other man was out of earshot.

She explained about Linco, adding, 'Nina is the daughter of Alistair's father's second wife. She and I met in Chiang Mai and Alistair asked me if I would come here with them. He feels she needs an older woman's influence. Her mother is rather...flighty and hasn't been much help to her.'

'You don't really fit the "older woman" category,' said Pete. 'I put you at around twenty-three until you said you and your ex-boyfriend were together three years and it's been a year since you split.'

'I'll be twenty-eight this year. To Nina that's middle-aged,' she said, smiling.

He surprised her by saying, quietly and seriously, 'She's a pretty but silly kid. You're a beautiful woman.'

No one had ever called her beautiful before and, although she didn't believe it, Clary was touched. 'Thank you,' she said, a little shyly.

At that point Fifi woke up and began to grizzle.

Pete rose with her in his arms. 'Maybe she had a bad dream. I'll go give her a wash and some juice. See you later.'

Clary finished the last few pages of her book and decided to change it for another. While she was in the village she bought herself a pair of trousers. They were of a similar pattern to the farmers' trousers she had seen in the night market at Chiang Mai; wide, cropped legs sewn to a deep band of material which folded round the hips and was tied in a knot at the waist. In Chiang Mai she had seen only navy blue trousers to match the working shirts. But someone supplying the stall here had had the bright idea of making them in vivid colours and pastels. Clary bought a pair in lime green, a garish colour in cool climates but great in the sun, with a tanned skin.

After changing her book at the buffalo skull library, she bought a couple of pineapple fritters hot from the wok on a stall in the beaten earth square and ate them on her way back.

She thought about Peter, forced by the loss of his wife to be mother and father to Fifi. Was it true, as Nina had suggested, that he and Clary would suit each other? Perhaps. He was a nice man. Most women could be happy with him. Probably she could be herself—if she hadn't met Alistair.

A few seconds later, after passing the Cabana spirit house and following the path where it swung to the left, she saw Alistair himself coming towards her. But he wasn't alone. Strolling beside him was a girl in a lilac swimsuit glittering with silver Lurex, with a diaphanous piece of purple and silver gauze knotted on one hip and partly concealing a pair of beautiful legs.

'Hello, Clary. This is Maria, my new neighbour. Clary is also staying at Ton Sai,' he said, introducing them.

Maria was a friendly as well as glamorous girl. An Italian, she spoke fluent English. She was on holiday with her sister and brother-in-law, who was a hotelier in Florence. They were all mad about snorkelling and for several years had spent their holidays on the coral atolls of the Maldives in the Indian Ocean.

'But I think I shall like it better here,' she said, smiling up at Alistair. Then her eye was caught by the splash of colour in the plastic bag Clary was carrying. 'Is that something pretty you have bought here?'

Clary showed her the trousers.

'Mm...I like them,' said Maria. 'Do they have them in my favourite colour?' She laid a hand on the top of her swimsuit. Her deep mauve-pink nails looked as if she had just come from the manicurist, and her gesture drew attention to her opulent breasts.

'I'm not sure. I know they have pink and pale green.'

'I must go and find out,' the Italian girl said eagerly. 'See you later, Clary. *Ciao!*'

As the sound of her animated voice, chattering to Alistair, died away behind her, Clary was swept by depression. She wouldn't be seeing much of him from now on, she thought forlornly. A lovely Italian who shared his enthusiasm for snorkelling was the perfect holiday companion for him.

Maria's farewell had reminded her of the waterside pizza restaurant at the Oriental Hotel and the trip on the river which had followed their lunch there. How lovely it would have been to go to the sea swallows' island, Phi Phi Leh, alone with Alistair, apart from the Thai boatman.

But Clary felt sure she had written herself off in his estimation by being a nuisance on the way down from the lookout this morning. And even if that hadn't happened, now the hut next to his was occupied by this lovely Florentine oozing sexual allure from every pore.

That night Clary was one of nine people making up a cosmopolitan supper party at Charlie's, a restaurant near the island's western beach. There were the three Italians, Nina and her Australian, a Swedish girl called Birgit who was staying in the hut next to

Joey's, Pete representing France and America and Alistair from the UK.

When Joey had asked if it was all right to bring along a Swedish girl student who had arrived that day and was on her own, Nina had looked rather put out. When she met Birgit she cheered up. The Swede was a strapping creature who clearly wasn't a rival.

They started dinner with a soup which was so fiery that half the party left most of it. Clary, who finished hers up, had numb lips for the rest of the meal, but felt that not being defeated by the peppery flavour redeemed her a little in Alistair's eyes.

Maria's sister and her husband were a vivacious couple who talked of little but food and had clearly been overeating for at least a decade. Maria would probably run to fat like her sister, thought Clary. But for the moment she was merely voluptuously rounded, her ripe curves displayed to advantage in an off-the-shoulder lace dress more suitable for a fashionable hotel than an island in the Andaman Sea. But none of the men would think that. They would only notice how feminine she looked.

She sat on Alistair's right with Birgit on his left. Clary sat between Pete and Luigi, who was festooned with gold chains and showed gold fillings whenever he roared with laughter, which he did a great deal.

It was a convivial evening which Luigi insisted on paying for, although everyone protested and wanted to split the bill. But, food being so cheap in Thailand, it probably cost him no more than dinner for one at his hotel in Italy, Clary calculated.

'I suggest that tomorrow we go to this other island,' he said, as the party broke up. 'What do you think,

Alistair? Wouldn't it be more amusing to go together...all of us?'

'I find Luigi a pain,' Pete murmured to Clary, walking back to Ton Sai.

'Oh, Pete, that's unkind! He means well.'

'He's a bore. Be honest, admit it.'

'Well...perhaps a bit of a bore.'

'Tomorrow will you have dinner with me...just the two of us?'

She wasn't sure how to respond. Was he asking her on a date? If so, she would have to refuse. There was no point in starting something with Pete which she couldn't finish.

Finding a reason to say no which wouldn't offend him was difficult. She was still searching for one when a Thai girl came hurrying towards them. 'Baby very sick, mister. We look for you...not find. Please come quick now!'

CHAPTER TWELVE

'COME with me, will you?' Pete said, over his shoulder, as he broke into a run.

'Of course.'

Clary was close behind him when he arrived at his hut, where two other Thai girls were trying to soothe Fifi's loud wails.

She stopped howling when she saw her father, but only temporarily. Although obviously comforted by his return, she was still a very unhappy little girl and almost at once began crying again, although on a less desperate note than before.

'She has a fever,' said Pete, after feeling her forehead. 'Get these girls out of here, will you, Clary? They've done their best, but now she needs peace and quiet!'

Fifi's baby-sitter and her two companions were all talking at once, explaining in their limited English what had been happening in his absence.

'Yes...thank you...you've been very good...not your fault Fifi not well...' Trying to be diplomatic, knowing how sensitive all Thais were to any hint of criticism, Clary shepherded them out of the hut.

Waiting outside was Alistair. 'Trouble?' he asked.

Considering that when Pete had been urged to come quickly Alistair had been strolling with the Italians, some way behind, it showed how observant he was that he'd noticed what was happening up ahead.

'Yes, the little girl isn't well. She looks as if she has a temperature. But it may not be serious. A tummy upset . . . a tooth. Children do get these fevers, I believe.'

Alistair nodded. 'So I've heard. Pete seems a competent chap. He'll know what to do. If there's any way I can help, I'll be in or outside my room.'

When she re-entered the bedroom and closed the door behind her, Peter had already removed Fifi's crumpled and sweat-soaked cotton nightie and was sponging her down.

'Did you throw up, honey?' he asked her.

She shook her head. 'It hurts, Papa.'

'Where does it hurt? Show me, *chérie*.'

But Fifi could only sob, 'It hurts . . . it hurts!'

'Everywhere, I guess,' said Pete, with a glance at Clary.

To Clary, who knew very little about small children's illnesses, his manner was reassuringly calm. Had Fifi been her child, she would have starting to flap in case it was something serious, something beyond the scope of the island's limited medical facilities.

No, that wasn't strictly true. There would be no need to flap while Alistair was within call. He would always know what to do, where and how to get help. Even more than Pete Albany, Alistair was a man who, merely by being there, made her feel safe and secure. She would never panic as long as he was around to take charge.

By next morning Fifi had developed a feverish cold but no longer complained of hurting and was able to eat a mashed banana for breakfast.

Pete, after a disturbed night, looked heavy-eyed and exhausted. He and Clary stayed behind when the others set out on the expedition to Phi Phi Leh organised by Luigi. Although the place on her head was no longer sore, and she would have been able to wear a mask hired from the dive shop at the Cabana, Clary felt that she might be needed to look after Fifi while Pete caught up some sleep.

With a cheerful face which belied her innermost feelings, she watched the boat party set off, Maria sharing a thwart with Alistair. This morning the Italian girl was wearing another shimmering bathing suit, red this time, with a gauzy piece of scarlet sari material, bought in the Maldives the winter before, she told Clary, while they were waiting for the boat to come and pick them up.

Clary liked the suit and the sari, but thought dangling gilt ear-rings and a gold ankle-chain with tiny bells tinkling on it was rather over the top for a boat trip. Perhaps she was just being jealous because the Italian girl had more panache than she had.

Later in the morning she played with Fifi while Pete napped on a lounger. It might be that, this evening, because the child wasn't well, he would ask the staff at the colony's restaurant to bring him some dinner on a tray. But sooner or later he would repeat last night's invitation for Clary to have dinner with him and she would have to have a gracious excuse ready.

There was little doubt in her mind that because he was deeply lonely and longed to be married again, Pete could quite easily learn to love her. But for Alistair, it could have been mutual. She and Pete had so much in common. In different forms, both had suffered the pain of loss. They had both opted out of the rat race. They both loved travelling and were keeping travel diaries. Although they were of different nationalities, in all the other important ways they seemed extremely well matched. Yet although she could become very fond of him, and probably enjoy making love with him, she did not and never would love him with the passion she felt for Alistair.

It was late afternoon when the boat party returned. Clary was on her verandah, reading and sipping iced water with a dash of Mekhong in it.

Experience had taught the boatman exactly when to cut the engine. The boat glided over the shallows and its bow came gently to rest on the shelving sand. Nina jumped out unaided. Luigi gave his large wife a helping hand and Maria stepped from the well on to the small foredeck and waited for Alistair to take her by the waist and swing her on to dry sand. She had the look of a girl who had thoroughly enjoyed her day and was looking forward to an equally enjoyable evening, thought Clary, with a pang.

All six of them came to the veranda to ask after Fifi and to describe the wonders of Phi Phi Leh. Only the picnic provided by the boatman had been disappointing.

'So tonight we must eat well,' said Luigi. 'We are going to try the Cabana restaurant. I will reserve a table. You and Pete will come, I hope, Clary.' He seemed to regard them as a pair.

She shook her head. 'Not tonight, Luigi. Another night, maybe.'

'Nina and I have a date in the village,' said Joey.

'But you, Alistair, you will join us?' said the Italian.

'I'd like you to have dinner with me—but not tonight,' replied Alistair. 'Later in the week, perhaps.'

He didn't explain why he couldn't eat with them tonight. Clary would have assumed that he had a date with Luigi's sister-in-law, except that Maria was looking noticeably crestfallen.

He remained beside the veranda while the others walked away.

'Are you eating with Pete?' he asked.

'No, he's having a tray in his room and I just don't feel in the mood for all that Italian vivacity.'

'Neither do I—and there's something I want to discuss with you. Shall we eat together in the village? There's nowhere one could describe as quiet and secluded, but the beach is quiet at night. We can talk on the way back.'

After her shower, Clary put on her new lime trousers and the black halter top she had worn to have dinner with Alistair the night of his arrival in Chiang Mai. What a long time ago it seemed; far longer than eight days.

What he could want to discuss had been puzzling her ever since he mentioned it. He had made it sound quite important. After racking her brains for an hour, she still hadn't come up with a likely solution.

She wondered why he had lost interest in Maria. Perhaps she had come on too strong and he didn't like that. Perhaps he hadn't been as interested as Clary had assumed. Not every man was turned on by big, bosomy, bedroom-eyed girls. Perhaps he was one of the exceptions.

They had arranged to meet in the reception area, and he was there before her, looking at the postcards for sale in the shop next to the reception desk while one of the staff hovered nearby in case he wanted to buy something. This girl was obviously longing to get back to the Thai soap opera on a small TV which was being watched by several other Village employees including the luggage-cart boy. Clary noticed with amusement the girl's relief when the tall *farang* turned away from the rack of cards, leaving her free to return to the television.

'Ah...the new trousers,' said Alistair, appraising Clary's outfit. 'They look better on you than they will on Maria. She has too big a backside for pants.'

This also amused her, but she didn't allow the reaction to show. It was unworthy to be pleased by his criticism of Maria's figure, but she couldn't help it. She had felt so downcast, thinking of him chatting up the Italian girl over dinner tonight. Instead of which he would be eating with her. Not, admittedly, with the object of chatting her up, but that didn't matter; merely to be spending an hour or two alone with him was enough to make her spirits soar.

Lights had been on in the huts occupied by the Italians when she passed them, so she knew they wouldn't be at a table in the Cabana restaurant when she and Alistair passed it on their way to the fishermen's village. Nor, when they reached it, did she see any sign of Nina and Joey, or of Birgit.

Alistair had already suggested they should eat at the restaurant, which had some outdoor tables, and this they did. There were no tables for two, so they took a table for four. After drawing out a chair facing the street for her, Alistair went round to the other side to seat himself.

'But you won't be able to see the passing scene from there. Why not sit on this side?' she suggested, indicating the seat beside hers.

'I'm very happy with the view I have,' he answered.

As she knew there was nothing to be seen behind her but the darkness, he could only be referring to her. She blushed with pleasure at the compliment.

Afterwards she had very little recollection of the meal itself, because she had been so intensely aware of her companion and of the need to be intelligent and lively company for him.

All too soon they were walking back the way they had come, but not at first by the beach, as Alistair had suggested earlier, because near the fishermen's village there were many boats moored and their lines would have had to be stepped over every few yards.

'When I got back this afternoon,' he said, as they began to walk back by the path, 'there was a telephone message from my secretary to say she had succeeded in locating Nina's mother. However, before I contact Aileen about Nina, I want your opinion of a new development. While we were out today, Joey and Nina told me they've fallen in love. Before you dismiss it out of hand, there are two points to consider. One is that Nina has told him about being in prison, and the other is that he wants to take her to Canberra to meet his family and perhaps to work for his elder sister who runs a riding school.'

'I already knew that Nina had taken a big shine to Joey. I'm glad she's told him about the prison. It suggests she's learned some sense from the experience.'

'Yes,' he agreed. 'I was pleasantly surprised to hear she'd made a clean breast of it. Joey's attitude is sensible too. He accepts that his parents won't approve of a marriage until he and Nina have known each other for at least a year, perhaps two. Even then they'll still be very young. Hence his proposal that Nina should work for his sister.'

'You're thinking that it sounds a better way to keep her on the rails than linking up with her mother?' said Clary.

'Precisely. I don't know Joey's parents, but they've been married a long time and sound good, stable people. I do know Aileen and wouldn't rely on her to look after a goldfish, let alone steer her daughter in the direction of a happy, settled future. As a mother, she's a proven failure.'

Clary said thoughtfully, 'I wouldn't like to bet that Joey's and Nina's present feelings for each other will last, but I can't see what harm could come of her going to Australia with him. And it might be the making of her.'

'Alistair... Clary... come and join us!'

Hearing themselves hailed, they looked to the right and saw Luigi beckoning them to his table in the outside part of the Cabana restaurant.

Alistair gave him a wave and a smiling shake of the head. 'Not tonight, Luigi.'

Sitting next to her brother-in-law, dressed to the nines, Maria was pouting. Clary knew how she felt. She had felt the same way herself when they went off this morning. It wasn't a fun experience, watching the man you wanted go off with another girl. But at least she hadn't let it show. And Maria didn't love Alistair. She wanted him because he was by far the most attractive man on the island. Clary loved him with all her heart. She wanted to make it up to him for being abandoned by his natural mother, losing his real mother and having to reject the advances of a wanton stepmother.

She wanted to give him everything a woman could give a man; to be everything he could want. A sympathetic listener to his problems. An exciting partner in bed. A loyal supporter in trouble. A quiet or amusing companion, according to his mood. A great cook. A welcoming hostess to his friends. A loving but sensible mother to his children.

She might never achieve perfection in all those endeavours, but oh, if she had the chance, how hard she would try!

A few minutes later, Alistair said, 'We can go the rest of the way by the beach. There are only few mooring lines to watch out for from here on.'

Once on the beach, Clary paused to slip off her shoes. Alistair was doing the same and rolling up the legs of his trousers, evidently intending to paddle once they had passed the last boat.

'What made you think I'd dismiss out of hand the idea of Nina and Joey's being in love with each other?' she asked. 'I should have thought that would have been *your* reaction.'

'At one time, yes, you're right. But some of my views have undergone radical changes,' he paused, 'since I've been in Thailand.'

What did he mean by that?

She was so busy trying to work it out that she didn't notice the line stretched like a trip-wire in front of her until it touched her shin and in a last-minute attempt to clear it, she almost fell over her own feet.

She didn't, because Alistair grabbed her, hooking an arm round her waist to stop her pitching forward on to the sand. Instead she lurched heavily against him and, the next moment, felt her suddenly pounding heart stop beating altogether as time and the world stood still.

CHAPTER THIRTEEN

'How can I dismiss the idea of love at first sight when it's happened to me?' Alistair said huskily.

In the half-light between the dark end of the beach and the brightness a hundred yards ahead where a spotlight was beamed at the water's edge, his blue eyes burned and sparkled as brilliantly as gems in a jeweller's window.

'...and not merely love at first sight...love at first sound. I fell in love with your voice...soft and conciliatory at first, and then angry...taking me to task from the other side of the world. I couldn't wait to see if your face matched your lovely voice. And it did! Oh, Clary...beautiful Clary...'

Both his powerful arms tightened round her, and then he kissed her.

He must love me, was Clary's first thought when, after an interval of only being able to feel, her mind began working again.

No one but a man in love could consider me beautiful. The first time we met he said, 'Be thankful you aren't a beauty.' Now he calls me 'beautiful Clary'.

He loves me. *He loves me.* HE LOVES ME! The exultant certainty of it spun round in her brain like a fiery Catherine-wheel throwing showers of bright sparks.

The next thing Alistair did was to let her go, but only in order to seize her by the wrist and lead her down to the sea, where, loping along in great strides which forced her to run to keep up, he headed for the section of the beach outside their huts.

Last night her lips had burned from the fiery soup. Now they tingled from his kisses, a much more pleasurable sensation. The pace he was setting was making her splash her new trousers, but she didn't care. What mattered except that he loved her?

She had sand between her toes and all over her feet by the time they came to the walkway outside his veranda.

'Sit down and I'll rinse your feet,' he said. Like her, he kept a couple of plastic bottles filled with salt water outside his door for that purpose.

Clary did as she was told and he sluiced the sand first from her feet and then from his own.

'Hang on—I'll get a towel.' He unlocked his door and disappeared. She heard his bare feet pattering across the grey and white bedroom floor tiles towards his bathroom.

Moments later he was back, the first person to dry her feet for her since her legs were so short they dangled when she sat on a chair. And after crouching in front of her to dry first one and then the other, her cupped a hand under her heel and pressed a kiss on her instep.

''Mmmm...' She gave a smothered murmur of pleasure at the warmth and softness of his mouth on the front of her foot, moving down towards her toes. 'Oh!' The exclamation came as he gently bit and sucked her sunburned, pink-pearl painted toes, as if they were delicious sweets.

Then approaching footsteps made him stop. Before she knew what was happening Clary was whisked into

his room and was once more held tight in his arms
while he kissed her softly on the eyelids and then,
hungrily, on her mouth.

Long pulse-racing minutes later, his searching
fingers found the knot at her waist and soon afterwards her Thai trousers slipped to the floor, leaving
her in the halter and a skimpy pair of micro-panties.

'How does this thing come off?' His voice was a
throaty growl that sent shivers of sensual excitement
down her spine.

Before she could answer his question, Alistair had
discovered that the stretchy black top could be pulled
upwards. Clary raised her arms to make it easy for
him to remove it. Seconds later the halter had been
cast aside and he was sitting on one of the beds and
she was perched on his lap with his hand caressing
her breasts, making her tremble with delight at the
gentleness of his strong brown fingers as he stroked
her as if she were an exquisite sculpture.

It baffled her that he could touch her with such
controlled delicacy when, swelling and pulsing against
her thigh, she could feel the urgency of his desire for
her. But he seemed to have iron control over his
feelings and to be determined to drive her insane with
longing before he unleashed his own passion.

At some stage of the night they got up and had a
shower together.

'I imagined doing this the day we arrived here,'
Clary told him, as they lathered each other.

'You did?' he said, looking surprised. '*I* did...every
time I had a shower. But I didn't imagine you having
those sort of thoughts. Whenever I let my feelings
show, you looked at me with your Ice Maiden

expression. It wasn't until you came belting over to Shark Point that I began to feel hopeful.'

'I thought you were having bedroom thoughts the night I had dinner in your suite at the Mae Ping.'

'Naturally. What man, if he's single, doesn't when dining with a desirable woman? But already I'd lost my heart to you. I can tell you exactly when I fell in love. I was standing in the lobby, wondering if you'd be on time, and you walked through the door and I thought, this is the one I've been waiting for all these years. Here she comes ... the girl I'm going to marry.'

'Oh, Alistair, you didn't really, did you? But you didn't know who I was. I mean, I could have been another girl ... not the one who'd telephoned.'

'I was pretty certain you were Clarissa Hatfield. The way you looked matched your voice. But if you had been someone else, Clarissa would have had to wait while I found out who you were and made sure there was going to be time to get to know you. A man doesn't wait until he's thirty-six for the right girl to show up to let her slip through his fingers.'

They had been talking in undertones so as not to disturb the sleep of their neighbours. Now silence fell in the bathroom until Alistair turned on the water, and as it sluiced the white lather from their brown bodies, they made love to each other.

Later, when they were dry, because the bed he had been sleeping in was now wildly rumpled, he took the cover off the unused twin bed and they lay down together, planning their future in whispers.

When, the next day, Clary told Pete that Alistair had asked her to marry him, he wished them well, but she sensed that there was disapproval as well as any dis-

appointment which might lie behind his outwardly
congratulatory manner. In spite of his shoulder-length
hair, she thought there were certain ways in which Pete
was more conventional than Alistair.

Ten days later, by which time Alistair was as darkly
bronzed as Thailand's sea gypsies, they flew back to
Bangkok and, at the airport, said goodbye to Joey,
who had changed his original plan and was going
home early to introduce Nina to his family. Alistair
had paid for her ticket and given them his blessing.

Whether the two younger people's long-term future
lay together it was impossible to predict, but Clary
felt that it might. As for her own future, all her earlier
doubts about whether someone like Alistair could care
for someone like her had been completely and forever
dispelled by the happiness of the days and nights which
had followed their first night together.

However, although Clary's hut hadn't seen much
of her for the remainder of their time on the island,
Alistair had booked two rooms for them at the
Oriental, and from tonight they would be sleeping
apart until they became man and wife.

'Little did I think, the first time we drove into
Bangkok, that next time we'd be holding hands,' she
said, as an airport limousine sped them in the direction
of the city's skyline.

'What's this?'

In the spectacular Cartland pink bedroom of the
Barbara Cartland Suite at the Oriental Hotel, an in-
ternationally famous film star looked with surprise
and puzzlement at the invitation card she had just
extracted from an envelope on her breakfast tray.

'"Alistair Lincoln requests the pleasure of your company at his marriage to Clarissa Hatfield in the garden of the Authors' Wing at six o'clock this evening, and to champagne and music on the terrace afterwards,"' she read aloud to her current companion, a handsome younger man she didn't intend to marry, having already been through several traumatic divorces.

'Alistair Lincoln is the head of Linco and the man behind Lincompute. Big bucks…mega-bucks,' he told her. 'I've never heard of Clarissa Hatfield. Sounds the sort of name the English upper crust give their daughters. She's not Lady Clarissa or The Hon. Clarissa, is she?'

'Not even Miss or Ms,' said the star, passing the card to him and turning her attention to the frugal breakfast which was part of the price of looking a youthful fifty, admitting to forty-five and being sixty next birthday.

'Will you go to this?' he asked.

'Why not? I've always enjoyed weddings, even my own. It'll make a break after a day of interviews and I'll enjoy the champagne twice as much if it's being paid for by Linco.'

The star had worked hard for her affluent lifestyle and sometimes she had to remind her companion, who had oodles of charm but no money, that it didn't grow on trees.

In the Kukrit Pramoj Suite, the first suite to be named in hour of a Thai literary lion, a famous singer and his wife were having a few days' rest en route to Australia where he was going to appear at a benefit concert in Sydney's Opera House.

'We've been asked to a wedding, here in the hotel this evening,' said his wife, in their native Spanish. 'Do you know this man Alistair Lincoln?'

'I think I have met him, very briefly, in London, but one meets so many people. I don't want to go to his wedding.'

'Then you rest and I'll go,' said his wife. 'I didn't have a proper wedding—we were so poor in those days—and I'd like to see this girl's dress. Clarissa...what a pretty name.'

'You may not have had a fancy wedding, but you have a husband who still loves you, thirty years later, and we're doing all right now, aren't we?' said the singer. 'Who would have thought in those days we should ever stay here?' he added, glancing round their luxurious bedroom.

'I always knew you'd be rich and famous one day,' said his wife. 'But I would have married you anyway,' she added, smiling at him.

In the Gore Vidal Suite, named after the American writer and TV personality who was a frequent visitor to Bangkok, a middle-aged English couple were resting after their flight from London.

'I still can't believe it,' said Bette Hatfield. 'Why would a millionaire—he must be a millionaire—want to marry Clary...Clarissa? She must have changed a lot since we last saw her. I mean, she's a nice girl, John, but she's never been pretty.'

'Not like her mother was, no. And you're still a damn good-looking woman, Bette.'

Holding a glass of champagne from the complimentary bottle awaiting them, with a 'Welcome to Bangkok' note from his prospective son-in-law whom they were to meet later, John Hatfield put his other arm round his wife's waist. He was taking to this unexpected taste of high living like a duck to water. His only worry was that the man his daughter was marrying might turn out to be older than himself. Still, what if he were? Better an old man's darling than a young man's slave, as the saying went. And although Clary had been a disappointment to them in many ways, her heart was in the right place.

If somehow—and how she had done it was hard to imagine—she had landed in clover, she would be sure to share it with her family. Perhaps he would be able to have a new car this year after all.

Unaware that her parents were in Bangkok, Clary was singing in the shower in the bathroom of Room 403. Alistair was in a room on the floor above.

Tonight, as husband and wife, they would share the Somerset Maugham Suite, but since their return to the Oriental the day before yesterday there had been little time for making love.

The rest of that day and yesterday had been a whirl of preparations for their wedding. The night before last and last night he had kissed her goodnight at her door, telling her to sleep well because on their third night in Bangkok they wouldn't be sleeping.

Most of the arrangements for the ceremony had been taken care of by Alistair, leaving her free to concentrate on her dress. At the Jim Thompson Silk Shop, where the most beautiful silks in the city were to be found, she had chosen a length of deep cream Thai silk which was being made up in a simple bare-shouldered style appropriate for an informal tropical wedding.

Yesterday afternoon they had taken a couple of hours off and gone to see the house where the late Jim Thompson—an American who after the second world war had revitalised the Thai silk industry—had lived on the bank of a *klong* in a building made of several traditional Thai houses and filled with art treasures. The place had had a peaceful atmosphere which Clary had found very soothing amid all the exciting bustle of preparing for her wedding.

Afterwards they had had an appointment to look at wedding and engagement rings in the jeweller's shop at the Oriental. The jeweller had already made a selection of rings made from fine quality stones in various styles and had advised Clary to choose her engagement ring first and the wedding band as a foil to it.

Her feeling was that the wedding ring which she would wear at all times was the more important choice. As she looked at the rings set with rubies and sapphires and the huge solitaire diamond he was displaying for her consideration, suddenly she knew that a wedding ring was the only symbol of Alistair's love she needed.

Turning to him, she had said, 'I really wouldn't feel comfortable wearing a ring worth a lot of money on my finger. They're lovely, but they aren't me. This is me——' showing the silver and moonstone ring bought in Bali which she was wearing on her right hand.

With commendable restraint, the jeweller had said, 'Charming, *madame*, but not, if I may say so, appropriate for all the occasions you will be gracing as the wife of Mr Lincoln.'

'When I'm Mr Lincoln's wife I shall still be myself,' she had answered, politely but firmly.

Alistair's comment had been, 'But, darling, you have such graceful hands. They deserve a beautiful ring. You needn't wear it every day.'

'Do *you* want me to have an engagement ring?'

'I want you to have whatever makes you happy.'

'It would make me very unhappy to wear a ring costing hundreds of thousands of *baht* and to remember a boy with twisted legs and a begging tin.' Sudden tears in her eyes, she had explained about the child she had seen, ending, 'Instead of buying me a ring, could you find him and buy him a future?'

And although the jeweller had looked at her as if she were mad, Alistair's response had been, 'Of course—if that's what you want, I'll look into it. You don't have to wear a wedding ring, if you don't wish to, you know. I shan't be wearing one.'

'No, but I'd like to.'

And so now, somewhere in Alistair's room, there was a finely plaited circle of two shades of gold and a band of platinum which, not many hours from now, he would place on her finger during the short civil ceremony conducted by the British Consul which was what they both felt was the right way to start their life together.

When Clary looked out of her window twenty minutes before her wedding, a neon sign in Thai script on the far bank was casting a ribbon of light over the rippling surface of the River of Kings. The vivid colours reflected in the water—cerise, purple, royal blue—were ones she would always associate with this exotic land, the last place she had expected to find love and happiness.

The discovery that her father and mother were in the hotel had come at lunchtime. They had been bowled over by Alistair, both of them obviously unable to fathom how she had captured such a man.

Listening to her father's rather sycophantic conversation with him, she realised that she didn't want to be given away in the traditional manner. Alistair had meant well by bringing her parents here and they would have been hurt had they not been invited. But she knew she had grown away from them during her travels; perhaps she had always been a changeling, not the kind of daughter they should have had. She must have some of their genes in her, but mainly she appeared to be a throwback to some unknown antecedent quite different from these two people who now seemed almost like strangers to her.

Hoping he wouldn't be too deeply offended, she had told her father it wasn't a conventional wedding. Alistair would escort her from her room to the garden.

A firm rap on the door indicated that this moment had arrived. Picking up the small spray of creamy orchids to match the chaplet of orchids on her hair, Clary hurried, smiling, to the door.

'They're so much in love, those two. Aren't you glad I persuaded you to come?' said the opera singer's wife.

'It's been better than some weddings I've been to,' he conceded.

The ceremony in the garden was over now and they and the other occupants of the hotel's suites, all of whom had accepted their invitations, were drinking champagne and helping themselves to delicious snacks artistically arranged on a buffet table at one end of the terrace normally occupied by the Ciao restaurant.

Tonight a notice at the entrance announced that the restaurant was closed for a private function and would re-open tomorrow. The tables, each with two metal containers beneath it containing the slow-burning coils which smelt like joss sticks and kept mosquitoes away, had been rearranged. Now most of the white marble floor was clear for dancing to music played by the string quartet which every afternoon played chamber-music in the Oriental's elegant lobby for guests having afternoon tea there. It was one of the hotel's traditions.

This evening, however, the musicians weren't playing sedate classical pieces but a succession of the West's most romantic melodies; music made for couples to dance to in each other's arms. The wife of the Australian grazier with a vast property in Queensland who had reserved the Wilbur Smith Suite for a two-day stop-over on a trip to Paris where she bought her clothes said, 'Remember this one, Harry?'

The grazier had no ear for music, but he knew enough about women, especially his Haze, to give her an affirmative squeeze as he danced her round the lily pool.

'Then you ought to know what it's called,' she said, with a beady look as she called his bluff. 'Fancy forgetting our song. How like a man!' Later that evening quite a number of long-married wives stood at the windows of bedrooms in the towering River Wing, watching the scene on the terrace below.

'The guests have all left, but the bride and groom are still dancing,' one of them reported to her husband, who was lying on the bed watching a war movie.

When his only response was an uninterested grunt, she sighed and resumed her wistful surveillance.

Held lightly in Alistair's arms, Clary knew that if they lived to celebrate their golden wedding, this evening, the beginning of their marriage, would still be a vivid memory fifty years on.

In the absence of relatives and friends, apart from her parents, it had been an amusing idea to invite the occupants of the other suites, and she had particularly enjoyed meeting the opera singer whose magnificent singing voice she knew well but whose equally melodious speaking voice she had never expected to hear speaking to her. The film star, too, had gone out of her way to be pleasant and was clearly a nicer woman in real life than the glamorous but bitchy characters she specialised in playing.

But of all Alistair's ideas for making their wedding special, the one Clary appreciated most was still happening. She guessed that at least a hundred of the men staying at the Oriental tonight had to be very rich, some even richer than her husband. But how many, if indeed any, of them would have arranged to dance long after the guests had gone?

'Strangers in the Night' played by a string quartet under a tropical moon... it was a dream come true; *he* was a dream come true. Knowing how extraordinarily lucky she was to be loved by a man with a romantic streak, she nestled closer and felt his arm tighten possessively round her, making her Thai silk dress rustle as he drew her to him.

HARLEQUIN
Romance

Coming Next Month

Available in March wherever paperback books are sold, or through
Harlequin Reader Service:

In the U.S.
P.O. Box 1397
Buffalo, N.Y.
14240-1397

In Canada
P.O. Box 603
Fort Erie, Ontario
L2A 5X3

Everyone loves a spring wedding, and this April, Harlequin cordially invites you to read the most romantic wedding book of the year

With This Ring

ONE WEDDING—FOUR LOVE STORIES FROM YOUR FAVORITE HARLEQUIN AUTHORS!

The church is booked, the reception arranged and the invitations mailed. All Diane Bauer and Nick Granatelli have to do is walk down the aisle. Little do they realize that the most cherished day of their lives will spark so many romantic notions....

Available wherever Harlequin books are sold.

COMING IN 1991 FROM
HARLEQUIN SUPERROMANCE:

Three abandoned orphans,
one missing heiress!

Dying millionaire Owen Byrnside receives an
anonymous letter informing him that twenty-six years
ago, his son, Christopher, fathered a daughter. The
infant was abandoned at a foundling home that
subsequently burned to the ground, destroying all
records. Three young women could be Owen's long-
lost granddaughter, and Owen is determined to track
down each of them! Read their stories in

#434 HIGH STAKES (available January 1991)
#438 DARK WATERS (available February 1991)
#442 BRIGHT SECRETS (available March 1991)

Three exciting stories of intrigue and romance by
veteran Superromance author Jane Silverwood.